THE KING OF TAOS

MAX EVANS

THE KING OF TAOS

A NOVEL

University of New Mexico Press Albuquerque

ISBN 978-0-8263-6164-6 (cloth)
ISBN 978-0-8263-6165-3 (electronic)

Library of Congress Control Number: 2020933522

Cover image Alan Currie | istockphoto.com
Cover and text design Mindy Basinger Hill
Composed in Adobe Jenson Pro, Kiln, Veneer, and Ashwood

IN THE BEGINNING

For my beloved and multitalented wife, Pat; our twin daughters, Charlotte and Sheryl; and for Patrociño Barela and Luz Martinez, great artists in wood during more than thirty years of creative time spent in Taos.

For Jan Haley and her husband, Gary; Embree (Sonny) Hale; Woody Crumbo, the younger; Sue Bason—all from or near my favorite small village in all the world, Hillsboro, New Mexico.

For Lorene Mills, Robert Nott, Johnny Boggs, Kirk Ellis, and David Smith—all from that gloriously beautiful and historic capital city of Santa Fe.

For writer and editor Stuart Rosebrook; Van Flaherty, PRCA stock contractor; fine friend, poet, musician, and author Andy Wilkinson; Jim Harris, museum director; and last, but certainly not least, Matt Thompson, Chris Pink, and David Marchiando, all lovers of our Galena King Mine.

AUTHOR'S NOTE
A BRIEF EXPLANATION OF THE *WHY* OF THIS LITTLE NOVEL

Quite some time ago, but only 120 miles north of this desk, a transition took place at the village of Taos and the ancient pueblo just north of town. I was there.

Amid a few world-remembered artists and those wishing to be so existed a small group of people who came together for a while, bonded by their mutual love of wine and talk.

We had moved from our little ranch next to the west mesa into town. We lived a block and a half south of the plaza, on both of the main routes the group used as they migrated individually to mesh together at the Sitting Place and the Lucky Bar, then later, sometimes—in two's or three's or altogether—they would gather on one route or the other. I couldn't help but observe them from my upper-story studio window. I became fascinated with their easy camaraderie and generosity with bottles of cheap wine. I knew there was a story here that I had to tell in fiction so I could get nearer to the fun of it all.

A year or so earlier, Dal Holcomb—a highly regarded and successful commercial artist, my first mentor in Taos, and a beloved friend and patron—had bought me a hat, a black cowboy hat, as a gift. Nothing too unusual there. I'd been a working cowboy kid—a real one—and even a cattle-ranch owner for a spell. After that I fulfilled my duties for a time as a combat infantryman in the hedgerows of France. What made that hat unusual was he'd bought it off a cowboy's head in a bar in Tucson, Arizona. It took a lot of ambition to get that accomplished, as a good hat is as important to a real working cowboy as a bat is to a ball player. Since my wife, Pat, and I both loved and respected Mr. Holcomb very much, I was obliged to wear his thoughtful gift.

So there you are. Shortly after I'd adjusted to another man's hat on my head I decided to inhabit the Lucky Bar and mix the best I could with the so-called winos. Oddly, the old black hat helped me be accepted in some way that I didn't bother to question. Then I found out that some folks somehow recognized me under the hat, and that they were clucking their little tongues and commiserating in a great show of sympathy to Pat about my fall from a partially respected author to a frequenter of a purely wino bar. The black hat had done it. It had served as a beacon to be observed as it entered the Lucky Bar, sometimes to vanish there for hours. Pat had to do her shopping through those conversations, but I was making progress in getting a novel implanted in my blood.

The lead for this historically inclined novel was a man I'd known before, whom I met when I developed some old mines with my pardner and art mentor, Woody Crumbo, the great Pottawatomie artist, on Bull of the Woods Mountain just past the famed Taos Ski Valley at the eastern end of Twining Canyon. The trail up to Bull of the Woods Mountain was exhausting to the point that the only way up was by foot or mule back. So I talked the Forest Service into surveying a trail so that, as I told them, one could drive a Cadillac car the twelve thousand feet up to the top. They did the survey, marking it with strips of red ribbon. Then the Forest Service asked us for eighty thousand dollars to build the road.

Since we had their professional survey and a bulldozer, I personally hired a man named Zacharias Chacon (for the purposes of this novel) to build the road. The first work was being done to install the Taos ski runs. At the same time we were trying to build around to our Bull of the Mountain mine. Zacharias kept a bottle of wine in the dozer's toolbox, and at lunch and at the end of the day he drank from it without trying to hide it. I said nothing because his was the only life in danger, and he seemed to know what the hell he was doing. He did. We built the road up there for twelve thousand dollars, and we did drive a Cadillac car right to the top. Our mines failed when the price of copper fell by half in just ninety days and we foolishly hadn't put any money aside to weather it all.

But that road invented the beginning of what is now a world-famous walking trail that goes near Wheeler Peak, New Mexico's highest, and back down near Frazier Mountain. The so-called wino Zacharias Chacon had done it. Not only that, but the walking trail helped bring patrons to Taos and, of course, to the ski run. So these two uphill, downhill sports and the art and artists of Taos have developed into an international draw that benefits all.

So this talented man who was indeed a lover of the grape had become my friend, always asking me, "Hey, Mr. Evans, when are we going back to the mines?" No matter what I told him he would say, "Just let me know, I'm always ready."

So there you are again. Zacharias, the untitled leader of the band-of-brother imbibers, paved the way, without a bulldozer, for my gaining membership and acceptance to live in some reality that led to this creation. I put some of it down in novel form in the late fifties and sixties during the time I had my first real creative burst writing *The Rounders*, *The Hi Lo Country*, and the three short novels in the collection *The One Eyed Sky*.

I'll never know why I didn't finish it. Maybe it was just too personal at the time. I don't know. I kept losing the manuscript, and finally, a million or so lives since, here it is for whatever it's worth. I found it and lost it ad infinitum, and magically to me, it's finally ready for publication.

Ol' Max Evans
ALBUQUERQUE, NM
SOMETIME IN THE TWENTY-FIRST CENTURY

1

ZACHARIAS CHACON got courageously out of bed. There was no way this large man could have a morning hangover. The grape was embedded too deeply in his being. He stood a moment, rubbed his proud face, and pushed at the long, thin hair on his head. His mind was made up. He headed for the water bucket, then he pulled a long drink from the dipper. In a moment it mixed with the grape, and he had his early-morning buzz. He stuck his hand in a pan and splashed a sprinkling of water on his face. He wiped this away gingerly, as if too much rubbing might give him a sore face.

Then he turned to Mama and said, "Mama, tell Rosita to get my mail. The check might come today."

Mama went right on ironing. This is how they lived, mostly. She ironed for ten hours a day and for other people. She raised her soft round face to him, and there was love in its brownness for a man who did no manual work and talked and drank his days away from home. He was always waiting for the check that didn't come.

Zacharias could do minor repairs on houses and barns as well as other sundry things such as mowing lawns. He felt that his meager earnings contributed to his family's survival.

He had injured his spine in the army during World War II, and five years back he'd applied for full compensation. He received one letter a year now. These he carried, wrapped in cellophane, in the pocket over his heart.

Every day his daughter Rosita went to the post office, and every day she came and hunted for him on the streets or in the bars to tell him, "It didn't come today, Papa. Maybe tomorrow."

Zacharias would look at her fine figure, with her long, dark hair and her large lips and her eyes like big black agates, and say, "It'll be here tomorrow. Si, mañana."

He walked over, then he picked up his little gray hat that turned up sloppily all around and put it carefully on his head. It had to be just right, for he wouldn't remove it until bedtime, more than likely. He put his thin-rimmed glasses on with some delicacy. He listened to his youngest children—aged three, four, and five—yelling outside. It was a comforting sound to him. Then he walked around behind the plentiful figure of his wife, took off his glasses, pulled her skirt up over her bounteous fanny, and cleaned his lenses. He looked at the big, naked bottom. *What a wonderful woman*, he thought, *all heart and ass*. He dropped the skirt, put on his glasses, and reached around her with his arms, clasping her breasts in a hug.

"Papa," she said, "I'll burn Mr. Braham's shirt."

"He has too many anyway."

Zacharias walked out without saying another word—with Mama it wasn't necessary.

"Well," he told himself as he walked along, "since its Saturday Romo will be on the plaza with his shine box." That meant he could probably acquire some money from his nine-year-old son. Saturday was a good day for shoeshine boys, and it was a good day for a man to have some money and some wine. He related this to himself until he reached the Resting Place. The Resting Place was really just a thick wooden rail to keep cars from bumping into Carlos's Liquor Store, but it served as a gathering spot for Zacharias and his amigos. The rail had been named by their friend Serapio Vargas, the Undertaker, who in turn received his moniker because of his obsession and love for anything to do with death. The Undertaker explained his feeling by saying, "We celebrate the birth of a baby entering this world, why not do the same when one departs?"

Tony the Indian was there, and he was already very drunk. Juandias, the Woodhauler, sat next to him, talking. Zacharias knew from past observation that Juandias only sat still where there was something to gain soon. That something made itself known instantly, as Indian Tony pulled the pint of Tokay wine from under his blanket and took a long drink. Then he handed the bottle to Juandias, who pushed the bill of his greasy little baseball cap to the side, rubbed his hand across his thick lower lip, blinked his wormy, little black eyes, and lowered the bottle a full third. He then handed it to Zacharias, who, without hesitation, left the bottle full of nothing but air—except for maybe a quarter inch in the bottom. Out of politeness Zacharias handed this back to the Indian, who fell off the Resting Place and broke the bottle. Tony did not bother to get back up. What was the use? There was no more wine.

"I'm expecting my check today," Zacharias said.

"That's good, amigo."

"Yes, that's good. We'll have a feast. I've already arranged for the goat, and we'll get Carlos to order, oh, maybe five hundred bottles of wine."

Juandias perked up at this, although he had no faith in the check. But it was such a fine dream—these five hundred bottles of wine—that he couldn't help but show some enthusiasm.

He straightened the dirty baseball cap and said, "Zacharias, you owe it to your old friends, those who've stayed with you through every trouble, to let them choose their own brand."

"You have something there," Zacharias said, feeling Indian Tony's wine tingle his skin. "Put in your order now, Juandias."

"No, it'll take some thinking. A matter of such vast importance must be thought about with much care."

"Don't take too long, because the goat is fat, and the check will be here today."

"In that case, I think I'll go in and consult with Carlos."

"That is right—seek the advice of an expert, I say."

Juandias went into the liquor store. Zacharias sat down on the Resting Place and pulled at Indian Tony's blanket.

"Get up, Tony. How do you think this will look to the tourists? Don't you know they've come a great distance to observe the colorful red man? How do you think this will appear to Mahatma Gandhi?"

Zacharias had no idea who Mahatma Gandhi was, but he liked the varying sound of words and knew that a man with such a name had to be important. Zacharias had always loved words. He had learned the most powerful muscles in the world are those of the vocal cords, causing on many occasions absolute embarrassment to the biceps and triceps. Which is the greater, he mused: the ability to pick up a large rock, or the ability with a few flips of the tongue to change the world?

Tony rolled over, slobbered, mumbled, sat up, then lay down on his back and slept.

Flavio Bernal strolled up. He looked like a miniature Rudolph Valentino. He always had his hands in his pockets, except for when he was grasping a wine bottle or a woman. Flavio was known as the Lover.

Zacharias was considerate, so he asked just the right question. "Did you get any last night?" The Lover almost did a jig. "It's not a matter of whether I did or not, it's a matter of who, and how many."

"Was it Juanita?"

"No, that was the night before."

"Emilia?"

"No."

"Alice?"

"She was one of them."

Zacharias raised his head. "One? There was more than one?"

"Of course. Last night was a good night. Guess who the other one was, Zacharias?"

"I give up."

"Then let me describe her to you, Zacharias." The Lover took his hands from his pockets and, with half-shut eyes, he moved them about, sculpting a woman in the air and trying to use the wording and emphasis that Zacharias would. He admired Zacharias's tongue even when it was used on him.

"She is about this tall," he said, holding his hand straight out from his shoulder. "Her hair is this long, and it smells of perfume, but gently, lightly, like a small breeze across a garden of roses. Her arms are slender but full of flesh. It is just the delicacy of the bones that causes this. Her lips are large and full of juice when she kisses. Her eyes are huge and dark, and they glisten like a tiger's when she makes love. Her waist can be reached around and held like this," and he cupped his hands in front of Zacharias's staring eyes. "Her legs are perfectly shaped as they blend into the ankles of a princess."

Zacharias was envisioning so clearly this imitation of his own speech that he was about ready to go home and interrupt Mama's ironing.

"And when she walks she sometimes shakes her head and her bottom at the same time, as if keeping herself aware that she's a woman."

"That sounds like my daughter Rosita."

"How did you guess it?" said the Lover, smiling and putting his hands back in his pockets, quite pleased.

"Well it had to happen sometime," said Zacharias. "It might as well be with a good amigo."

"The trouble is, Zacharias my friend, she wants to get married. I'm going to depend on you to talk to her for me."

"It is all right for you to make love with her, but I forbid you to marry her."

"I have no worries then?"

"I will give her a father's advice when she brings my check today." Zacharias felt the thirst come again. "Do you have any money today, Lover?"

"No, Emilia hasn't sold even one bowl of chili. But by the afternoon I'm sure to have some."

"The saints may call for us before then. What kind of woman is this Emilia? How could she be so cruel?"

"She's not cruel. She works all day in the little restaurant. When she has money, it is mine. And when I have time I give her love in return. You mustn't criticize Emilia. She's a fine woman. A generous woman as well as a fine lover when she is not worn out from her duties."

"I'm sorry. It's just this October sun. There's something about that sun that creates thirst. Maybe it is because all summer it has soaked into these old adobe walls. Or maybe," Zacharias stepped forward a couple of steps to get a better look down the street, "it is the reflections of the golden leaves on the cottonwoods and aspens. Who is so wise as to know these things? All the same, October has a very thirst-making sun."

"That is true. I've noticed this occurrence for the last seven years."

The Lover went looking for a new love, and Zacharias strolled reluctantly toward the plaza. His dislike had nothing to do with its appearance. It was simply that if he was on the plaza, he was broke. Otherwise he would be in a bar on skid row.

He stood a moment to give the area a true eagle-eye survey. Everything seemed to be normal. A few blanketed Indians were bunched in a group on the east side of the plaza, watching some tourists drive around looking for a place to park. They soon found one, and they got out of the car, stretching, talking, and looking in all directions. Then some started wandering in and out of the galleries and shops, while the rest posed in front of the plaza's historical marker and took pictures of each other.

Zacharias's attention was focused at the moment on spotting his son Romo and then waiting until he saw him at work on someone's shoes. This was his lucky day. He had only stood behind the post four or five minutes when he saw Romo bending down in front of the La Fonda de Taos Hotel with the shine rag flying. He was working fast and hard because he wanted to go see John Wayne in a good shoot 'em up.

He eased around and leaned against the building behind Romo. He watched carefully as a big fat tourist with a big fat cigar shifted from one foot to the other. He could tell this was some sort of four-flusher. He'd probably not tip at all.

The man said, "Here, son, that's a good job." And he handed Romo a whole dollar.

Zacharias was very pleased that his judgment proved wrong.

Romo looked around quickly, knowing that many Saturdays his father relieved him of his money. This afternoon he wanted to go to the picture show and stuff his belly full of popcorn and cookies.

Too late! He felt the large hand on his shoulder. Without a word he handed the dollar to Zacharias.

"Come with me, Romo."

Together they walked around the plaza and over to the Lucky Bar. They entered to the bittersweet smell of ten thousand spilled drinks and the open urinal behind—which, for some reason, was a poor target.

Chaco, the proprietor of the Lucky Bar, knew that business was on hand, no matter how small. Zacharias had entered with a purpose.

"What'll it be?"

Zacharias studied the back bar. They both knew it would be the same Tokay wine as always, but the ritual must be maintained.

"Give me a glass of Tokay," he said, slapping the dollar bill proudly, almost boastfully, on the bar.

He downed half the glass, and when Chaco gave him the change he handed a dime to Romo and said, "Here, son, go buy yourself some candy. You've earned it."

Little Romo pushed his hair back from his forehead, stuck the dime deep in his pocket, picked up his shine box, and got the hell out of there.

"Did you see that, Chaco? I don't know what's going to become of this younger generation. That boy didn't even say thank you. Just took his papa's money and ran."

"We spoil them too much," said Chaco, who had eight half-hungry kids of his own.

"That is right," said Zacharias. "We give them too much. We're too generous."

"That's right," he said, and he drained his glass of wine, tasting it to his very toes.

2

HOW COULD THERE BE SO MUCH SKY *in the entire world,*
the twelve-year-old Kansas stock-farm boy asked himself as he gazed
hypnotically at the majesty. He sat in the front seat of a car that had just
topped out above the horseshoe on the Santa Fe highway. His father
had purposely driven into the bar ditch as the vastness of the valley
suddenly appeared before them. They stared, but young Shaw Spencer
absorbed. His father leaned forward from the front seat and adjusted
his wire-rim glasses. Taos village and the thousand-year-old Indian
Pueblo just past it were miniscule patches trying to climb the massive
blue-timbered mountains to the north. "That's some kind of scenery,"
the boy's father said as he slowly drove the car back on the highway and
down toward the ancient village.

It was the only vacation they'd been on since young Shaw had been
born. They had seen the great white sands of southern New Mexico
and marveled at the vast white ocean and all the formations of mesas
and distant mountains surrounding it. Their budgeted schedule only
allowed a couple of circles around the famous plaza of Santa Fe before
heading on to Taos. The elder Spencer had spared the vacation money
so they would have the next full day in Taos. Berta, his mother, had
insisted on this because of her son's growing interest in art.

It was mid-afternoon before they got fully checked into the motel
only three or four blocks from the plaza on the Eagle Nest highway.
There was a long block of galleries and curio stands one block before
the plaza. The plaza, where the flags of several nations had flown,
revealed a world of true magic to young Shaw. He was, in fact, in an
utter state of wonder, feeling a sense of reverence almost. He hadn't
been born here, but he wished ardently that he had. The paintings

and the sculpture held such allure that he was possessed by feelings of which he had no knowledge. The Spanish-speaking people, the colorfully blanketed Indians, the adobe buildings and homes all seemed as foreign as the other side of the earth. Yet he felt as if he'd always been here. His hereto unknown emotions kept him awake the whole night. It didn't matter. Who needed sleep when his entire body and mind seemed to be whirling in a velvet cloud of reverence? He whispered into the little room made of mud bricks, "Oh, Great Mystery in the Sky, move me here please. This is where I belong. I feel it all over. I know it, Great Mystery. I must live and die here. I must."

The same vast desert that surrounded him, which the occupants of the Kansas car stared at in awe, was simply *there* to Zacharias Chacon. His family had been here for hundreds of years. The wonderfully colored sagebrush over all this land had once been grass that fed the thousands—hundreds of thousands—of sheep. That was before the longest drought on record, when the once wealthy and powerful had kept on overgrazing until the sagebrush took over and the once dominant ranchers were replaced by artists because of it. But none of this was on his mind as he neared the village of his blood and the soul of his ancestors.

He could hardly wait to be with his family, and he made a deep vow to himself that he would never leave Taos to drive the machine again. He wouldn't have to, because he was due years of back pay for his wound from the war. The check had probably come in the mail today. He would buy his own bulldozer and work for the people of Taos, even the crazy artists.

Zacharias shifted gears, controlling the mighty steel blade on the D8 Caterpillar with the delicacy of a classical violinist fine-tuning a Stradivarius violin. It was as natural to him as drinking water. Here on Mt. Wilson north of Grants, New Mexico, he worked happily at the highest-paying job he'd had since the end of World War II.

His late father, José Chacon, had driven a road grader for almost twenty years for the county of Taos. Zacharias had barely been out of diapers when his father held him on his lap as he smoothed the dirt roads and graded the drainage ditches on each side. In only a few years he was able, sometimes, to drive the heavy machine by himself while his father visited and shared a nip of wine with one of his little army of friends. Dirt-road fixers have more friends than most. Zacharias had learned the gears, the sound, the feel, the very essence of heavy machinery by the time he was in high school.

Soon the greatest of wars infected the world. He had spent only a year at Highland University, which stood south across the mountains in Las Vegas, New Mexico, before he decided to join up and help free the world. In what seemed but a few minutes later he was driving a bulldozer for a construction battalion in Normandy. Since his maternal grandmother had been German, Zacharias wondered if it was a sin to kill the enemy. Soon it wouldn't matter. The success of the beachhead invasions stalled. The thousands of little farms and pastures, surrounded by hedgerows made of rock fences, dirt, and branch roots, made an almost impregnable fortress. The Nazis were experienced in their murderous game of chess. They dug holes in the corners of the farms' hedgerows and installed machine guns that could cover two fields at once. The men, and sometimes German children, were given orders to fire at the enemy until they ran out of ammunition or lost their lives. They knew as well that when the Allied tanks tried rolling over the hedgerows, their more fragile bellies were exposed and were knocked out of action. So with this knowledge the Nazis outmaneuvered, outgunned, and ultimately stopped the mighty Allied army's advance in its bloody tracks.

This massive problem was solved by a sergeant in Zacharias's battalion. He simply asked a supervisor if maybe they could use the iron stakes from the beaches by welding some in a V-shape on the front of the bulldozers and work through the hedgerows without exposing the underbelly of the allied tanks. To everyone's surprise, after some testing and adjustments it worked. Zacharias was one of the first to knock a passage through the hedgerows. Now the Allied tanks could simply drive through, with small arms and cannons firing, opening the way for the infantry to advance. The infantry broke through at Saint Lô, France, and the war would be much shorter, with far less blood torn and ripped from flesh—though the bullets still zipped all around, and the artillery hounded the soldiers and terribly abused the earth and air. Zacharias somehow escaped whole, but his luck changed on a day of celebration.

One of America's favorite singers, Dinah Shore, was performing for the troops a couple of miles from the front lines. He could hardly believe it when he and an army truckload of men were chosen to go back from the front for an entire day and hear one of the world's great entertainers. What luck! What joy! What a day! He was in the back of the truck nearing his destination when the vehicle hit a hidden hole, and Zacharias Chacon of little Taos, New Mexico, fell out with a jolt and cracked a bone in his lower back. He was hospitalized. He mostly recovered from his wound, but he did occasionally feel stiffer, and he would still experience pains from the fall, and he sometimes needed to wear a wide belt to ease the pain.

The two atomic bombs that were dropped on Japan to end that terrible conflict had led to his work at the foot of Mt. Wilson, near the town of Grants in west central New Mexico. He felt the blade cut through the overburden to the host rock below and uncovered a blade-wide swath thirty or forty yards long. Then he spun the machine to do the same in the opposite direction. He was laying bare the large formation of earth pigmented with yellow cake, the oxidized form of uranium.

There was a small army of these dull yellow monsters working here to uncover the millions of tons of earth to make a concentrate of the deadly ore. The metal mill under construction a mile below was almost finished. The race was on to possibly blow up most of the earth's surface and everything on it. And he and the other workers were unanimously part of it. The pay was good and the work fit all, especially Zacharias Chacon of Taos, New Mexico.

Oh, the clock of nature in his head told him it was lunchtime. That same clock had informed two of the other drivers, for they were already walking to the spot with grass and trees that they left ungraded each day to better enjoy their lunch. Zacharias killed the engine and dismounted from his iron steed, lifted the lid on the metal toolbox attached to the dozer, and took out his little box of sandwiches and his little grocery sack containing a bottle of the grape.

The three men ate their sandwiches, visited, and stared proudly out at their morning's work. Zacharias finished his tortilla, lamb, and green chile sandwiches with much satisfaction and took a long pull at the bottle of wine to complete the well-deserved repast. He offered the quart bottle of red to his companions. They politely shook their heads no. Then they each lit a cigarette, one offering a smoke to Zacharias. He said, politely, "I don't smoke." They all three saw the jeep working its way up the graded foothills toward them. It stopped, and the assistant manager of the project alighted from the jeep, only several yards away, and walked purposely up the hill. "Gentlemen," he nodded. They all spoke or nodded at once and stood up, knowing the lanky, long-nosed, bespectacled official had not arrived for a simple greeting. Without thinking anything of it Zacharias offered him the three-quarter-full bottle, saying, "It was a dry drive out here, no?"

"Mr. Chacon, put the bottle away. I'm here to give you notice. Homestake Company does not allow drinking on the job. None. You can pick up your check at the office in town." He turned and walked swiftly over the graded earth, moved back to the jeep, roared the engine, and drove back down the slope in some kind of satisfaction.

Zacharias hadn't had a chance to utter a word of protest. He stood there holding the bottle and said softly, more to himself than his dismayed companions, "But I always had a drink with my lunch . . . when I worked for Molly mines at Questa, and . . . and . . . no one ever said a word to me . . . my work was so good . . . always . . . the same at Bull of the Woods Mountain . . . I . . ."

Zacharias was a man of acceptance. He shook hands with his two fellow drivers, unaware that one of them, jealous because Zacharias delivered a third more work than him every single day, had turned him in.

He walked with some pride across the ground of his day's work. He kissed the engine cover, patted the machine like a favorite dog, and strode proudly downhill to his old pickup. He started thinking about his wife, Lisa, whom he called Mama, and his five children back in

Taos. He would see them before midnight with three weeks' pay in his pocket. The world was going to be joyous at their togetherness again. He did a little dance, a jig of sorts that he always did when he was happy or, rarely, depressed. His original dances, always different, could not be described except for their spontaneous agility.

But it turned out the payroll clerk was gone until morning, so he spent another night in Grants. The next morning he got his check and went to the bank and cashed it. He didn't want a bank in Taos to even look at the company check. Besides, the cash felt good in his pocket.

He stopped in Española and had a fine hot lunch of that wonderful hot chile made nowhere else in the world but northern New Mexico. He drove on toward Taos through the canyon alongside the Rio Grande. And there was the big horseshoe in the highway. He topped out and looked down the expansive Taos Valley. Home. He slowed for a car pulling out on the road with a Kansas license plate. He decided to drop back and let the Kansas car lead him on to Taos.

Everyone in the world should be blessed to see such a pageant. The mighty valley undulated down, down, to the great gash through the volcanic rock. It had surely taken millions of years for the river to create such a passage during its more than eighteen hundred miles through vast deserts and patches of green to the Gulf of Mexico. Uncountable numbers of sagebrush carpeted the valley and cast a pale blue-green color that had enticed the pioneer artists to the Taos area in the first place.

And then there was the other half of one's total vision from this special spot . . . the sky. No. There were seven skies, each with different shaped clouds and diverse angles and colors of the sun's rays. The seven skies of Taos were so massive that they contested with the earth below.

3

AT THE VERY INSTANT Zacharias drained his glass, Shaw Spencer, a newcomer in town, stepped into the First State Bank of Taos and deposited $3,600.18. It was the last money from the last crop of hay he'd ever own. He felt rich. His prominent Adam's apple jumped up and down at the prospects of this new life. He could get by for two years if he was careful—and if his pictures started selling, which he certainly expected they would. He just might make it big—real big—before the two years were up.

He pushed the fall of brown hair from his forehead, clamped his jaw tightly, squinted his large hazel eyes, and left the bank to begin his conquest of Taos and the entire world of art.

Just getting here completed the vow he'd made over a decade ago when the twelve-year-old and his parents had vacationed through here and he'd fallen so in love with the ancient village that he'd sworn to return. He had. He was here. He took a deep breath of air, reveling in the adobe, piñon, and sagebrush, in the unique scent of the Taos world. It was in his blood now forever.

He rented a little three-room mud house a long block from the Taos plaza. It didn't have an indoor bathroom, but it did have water piped in. That was better than he'd had on the farm. Part of the floor had rotted and collapsed, but he fixed that by filling the cavity up with dirt and packing it hard with the shovel blade. He hung his seven and a half pictures, and then he went to a secondhand store and purchased a single bed, two wooden chairs, and an old couch that had cotton oozing out here and there, like mud squeezed from between fresh-laid adobe. It was home, and he would improve on it as time passed, he figured.

His next stop was the art store. He introduced himself to the lady there. This was a laughing lady—the kind who laughs at everything and nothing.

She asked him, her eyes taking repeated inventory of him, "Are you—ha, ha—a visitor—ha, ha—or permanent?"

"Permanent. I'm an artist, and I came here to paint."

"Oh, you'll—find this a—delightful place—to paint. So—quaint, you know."

"Yes, it is different—all these adobe houses, crooked streets, mountains, Indians . . ."

"Yes, it is different—so—quaint. Now what—can I do for you?"

Shaw said, "Well, first I'd like a tube of ultra-marine blue."

She repeated it after him, "A tube of ultra-marine blue."

"And then six yards of canvas, high-grade linen, please."

"Six yards—high-grade-linen canvas." She measured, cut, and tied a string around the roll of canvas then looked at Shaw through her glasses. The permanent laugh lines deepened behind her perfumed makeup as she smiled broadly and said, "Is that all?" and then the smile changed to a sort of jerking laugh again when he handed her the cash. Later he would have occasion to witness this smile eradicated from her face like copper in acid, and the color left behind would be the same. Green.

He stretched six canvases, put one on the easel, and got out all his paints and brushes. The searing fires of creation pounded in his veins as he stared hard at the blank whiteness. He stared and stared.

"Now just what in the hell am I going to paint?" he said aloud to himself. "I guess I need a model, or maybe I should go out into the glorious countryside or the picturesque streets of Taos and sketch first. I need to know the streets of Taos and sketch first. That's it! Yes, that's what I'll do. I need to know the land, feel it in the most sensitive marrow of my bones. Association with those whose dedications are the same as mine is what I need, and to feel their inspirations seep into the spirit and inspire me to flaming fame." Without realizing he was speaking to himself in unnatural sentences, he quickly gathered up his pencils and sketchbook, settled himself in the pickup, and drove out north toward the Taos Indian pueblo.

But upon arrival there he found so many onlookers, both tourist and Indians, he was embarrassed to stop and sketch. He could accept praise, and even attention, but not at this serious moment. He then drove south to the village of Talpa, one of the many tiny suburbs of Taos. There was quite a lot of traffic on the highway, so he decided to get out and walk into the brush rather than have the eyes of foreigners on him as he followed his life's work.

Finally he came to the edge of a stream. It was perhaps four feet wide, and it rippled along at six or seven inches at the deepest. He tried to sketch the ripples and waves as he saw them. After an hour or so of this, his sketch pad was full of wavy lines that looked much more like the hind leg of a zebra than an enchanting mountain brook.

He turned to a clean page and moved on down the creek bank. A clump of sagebrush, almost perfectly balanced on one side, caught his eye. *Very picturesque*, he thought, and he started to draw it. He looked at it again and drew some more. If there was ever a pile of brush heaped at random by a tree trimmer who hated his job, this was it. He folded up his sketch pad and went to the pickup. He had to face it. He was an amateur in spite of his studies in Chicago.

On the way back to town, he saw a sign—THE SAGEBRUSH INN. Since this particular shrub was prevalent in his thinking, he drove the pickup into the driveway and alighted. His young spirits needed reviving. He must associate with one of his own, and surely this was just the place. The land was not enough.

The lobby of the Sagebrush Inn was filled with southwestern atmosphere and the smell of piñon wood burning in the fireplace. A huge north window looked out on the Sangre de Christo Mountains, the adobe walls were hung with paintings by some of Taos's finest, and the floor was resplendent with Navajo rugs of every design. Shaw ambled around, soaking up the paintings. There was a Berninghaus, a Blumenschein, a Couse, and some he'd never heard of. Their evident professionalism made him feel even more amateurish and afraid, and yet there was that thrill there just under the skin, singing to him, "You'll do it, Shaw, someday. Yes, you will. You'll be one of those hanging there."

His wanderings took him to the cozy little bar just off the corner of the lobby. He entered.

"Hello there," came a singsong voice from behind the short bar.

"Hi," Shaw said.

"What can I do for you, my laddie?" the man asked in a voice both American and resident British.

"Well, I don't know exactly," Shaw said.

"Whiskey, a cocktail, or beer?" The excitement of all those wondrous paintings had Shaw's mind somewhat addled. He slid hesitantly onto the barstool and said, "Oh, just fix whatever you like best," which showed he was as inexperienced at drinking as he was at painting.

"Well, my laddie, that will be no trouble at all." He paused and asked, "You are over twenty-one, aren't you?"

Shaw laughed softly and said, "Not by many moons, but enough. You want to see my driver's license?"

"No, you have an honest face. Besides, I can usually tell if people are lying about their age. I'm Gene Atkins. I tend bar to pass the time while I prepare to start my novel."

Shaw watched Gene—with his huge hook nose, thin mustache, and hands of a rock mason—mix the scotch and water. With a flourish he set the drink down in front of Shaw and stared at him from mischievous blue eyes. He liked Shaw's neat appearance, his quiet brownish eyes, and his thick auburn hair with the unruly locks that kept falling over his forehead. Yeah, not a bad-looking kid. Six feet, sturdy muscle, and just the right amount of stubbornness in his face.

"Passing through?"

"No, I've just moved here."

"Oh, from where?"

"Kansas. I had part interest in a stock farm near the Panhandle. Been away from it for two years studying at the Chicago Art Institute. When I got back I sold my cattle, and now I've come here to paint."

"A painter, eh?" Gene the bartender already figured that this young man had sold a large cow ranch, which he'd no doubt inherited from a rich Texas uncle. "I'm a writer myself . . . just tending bar here to pick up a bit of atmosphere. You know how 'tis?"

Shaw wondered if Gene was sincere about writing, even though he'd already told him twice in less than a minute that he was a writer.

"Seems like a good place to get it—just from what I've seen in the short time I've been here."

"Well, it has a certain fascination about it . . . a certain complexity . . . uhmmm, a certain pettiness, which you'll learn firsthand, I regret to say, after you've been here awhile."

"I come from just outside a small town. I loved it."

"Well, I venture to say that you'll find this a very different small town here. There's a little bit of most of the world here—by that I mean so many nationalities intermingled, assorted creative talents harmonizing and clashing, and all sorts of separate clichés, kooks, aristocrats, oh, you call it. Anyway all these naturally produce a completely wild range of thoughts, actions, situations, what have you. Get the picture?"

Shaw half cleared his throat, having received more information than he needed or wanted, and said, "Sounds pretty complicated."

"Oh, well, I'm probably confusing you with this thumbnail description. Can't be described properly like that, that's why I've been trying for five years to write a book about it."

"Oh, I see."

Shaw ordered another drink, and Gene looked at the clock hanging behind the bar and commented, "Four o'clock, Julie should be arriving any moment." Just as he was about to make further comment, a young woman walked in and spoke.

"Hi, Gene."

"Haaaa," Gene said jokingly, "late again, my dear." There was a fondness in his voice, and his face brightened. "Shaw, this is Julie. She's been working here temporarily, to quote a tragedy. Just something to do while stopping over on her way to the west coast. Julie, this is Shaw, a newcomer here. He's a painter—I might add a rich one, just sold a cow ranch." Gene winked at her. "And . . . he is unmarried." He then gave Shaw a questioning look to see if his statement was correct or not.

Julie nodded and smiled slightly at Shaw. He really wanted to tell them he'd sold only a few mangy old range cows and no land at all, but then it did feel good to be thought rich. Hell, this might be as close as he'd ever come to it, and he'd better make the most of it.

By the cocktail hour, Shaw had moved down a stool so he was next to Julie's stand at the bar. He had made a complete inventory of her . . . deep-blue eyes, skin as smooth as a milk bottle, movements as limber as an overused bedspring. Her teeth showed a little too much when she smiled, and the inside of her upper lip showed a little. Shaw immediately wanted to kiss her. But it was nearly two o'clock in the morning before this came about.

It became more and more evident that Gene had a great desire for Julie, but circumstances—including a wife and two children home from school for the summer—prevented him doing anything about it. Moreover, it was his wife's money that gave him the time and privilege of calling himself a "writer"—something he desired even more than Julie.

Gene was very expansive as Julie warmed to Shaw. It was definitely a weird way of looking at it, but he figured if he could get them married he might still have Julie on occasion. Taos was always overrun with dreamers.

Shaw was buying drinks now for everyone who came into the bar. Gene introduced him to Dal Holcomb, a bald-headed, gray-bearded commercial artist who was casually dressed in a grayish-brown sports jacket and a bright-yellow knit shirt. Shaw decided he looked the part perfectly of a successful, slightly jaded, boozing commercial artist. Dal was a jovial fellow, partially because he was knocking down well over forty grand a year doing magazine illustrations and advertising for a big New York agency. Their friendship was immediate and mutual after Dal found out Shaw was a struggling young artist—even if he was very rich. He dashed out to his convertible and returned with a mandolin, which he played with much spirit. Shaw thought it was magnificent and didn't hesitate to proclaim it over and over.

Shaw drank the scotch rapidly, and if he hadn't felt Julie's arm caressing his waist he would have gone to sleep standing up just like a horse. Instead he shook hands with Dal and Gene and then stumbled out with Julie to her room in the back of the inn.

They were hardly outside when Shaw grabbed her and said he loved her about twenty times. All the while he wanted to shut himself up by kissing that obscene pair of lips. It took about three wrestles around the room and two falls over the couch before he could get her on the bed. But that knot in his jaw was set.

Julie said, "No, no. Yes, yes," right into his mouth, and she pushed and twisted and then spread her legs and screamed as he entered, hollering as loud as she could, "Priest! Priest! I want a priest!"

Shaw thought, *What the hell does she want a middle man for? In moments like these one should go straight to the top.*

The next morning Shaw was surprised to find himself home alone. He got up an inch at a time, looked for a cigarette, and couldn't find one. During the search he discovered that he only had twenty-six cents left in cash. He'd have to go to the bank and make another withdrawal.

He stared again at the blank, white canvas. For a moment he thought it was tinged with pink. Had he painted an undercoat the day before? He couldn't recall. He looked again, and the canvas was as white as ever. It must have been the scotch filtering through his bloodshot eyeballs that turned the canvas pink.

He felt far too bad to cook breakfast; besides, huevos rancheros were the only thing that would give him the will to live. He half stumbled to the pickup and drove to Spivey's Cafe on the Colorado highway. He felt dizzy and silly and ashamed. Here he was a painter, and the only way to graduate to that electable position known as "artist" was to paint. This thought and the first taste of the eggs and tostados drenched in pungent chile sauce gave him a momentary surge of energy. His pad and pencils were still in the pickup, so when he finished his breakfast he drove out to the west of town along a winding road. He saw a skinny old horse standing with its head down. He sketched.

The lines blurred together, but he worked on. By god he had to. Suddenly he jumped out of the pickup to heave. It left him weak, and even in the warm sun he felt the perspiration bursting out and coldness come over him. He got back into the pickup and stared straight ahead for a while until the world quit tilting and bending around like a TV picture gone bad.

Feeling a fraction better—which is to say he could move—he picked up the sketch. It wasn't bad. Not bad at all. He suddenly thought of Julie, Gene, and Dal Holcomb. His friends. His girl. He wanted them to see this sketch. Then he wouldn't have to be rich to be someone. He could show them he had talent, and they would love him just for that. They might even respect him. Oh, great world!

He hurried the pickup toward the Sagebrush Inn.

"Haaaa," Gene greeted him with a gleam of trickery in his eye that Shaw mistook for one of deep admiration.

Julie lit a cigarette and said, "Good afternoon, darling," blowing smoke as if it were the soul of man.

The hangover was dismissed. He was sure they, too, felt his exuberance.

"I've been working this morning. Look," he said, "just look!" They did.

"That's nice," Julie said casually.

"Not bad," Gene said.

Shaw's spirits dropped below his knees, but just at that moment Dal Holcomb entered.

"Let me see what you have there, Shaw Boy." He held it out away from him and squinted, his eyes half-closed, "Huhhh, huhhh." He continued to look. "It has feeling."

"The drinks are on me," he said suddenly. "This is my boy. He'll be the next news from Taos."

Shaw melted with emotion, pulled out the three hundred dollars he'd withdrawn from the bank, and said, "Let's celebrate."

Dal repeated the statement. He'd left his mandolin home, but this made no difference. Some spoons borrowed from Gene furnished the music. As the party gained momentum, Dal slid out into the small empty space on the floor and did a soft shoe from a time so far back that, to a young squirt like Shaw, the dance was now misty.

New people kept coming in and out of the bar, but Shaw paid no mind. He was rich, rich, rich. He was overloaded with friends—more friends than he knew what to do with—a famous artist praising his work for its promise, a beautiful girl that he loved with all his heart, and an intellectual bartender tending to his every need. Gene beamed on him as if he were a younger brother. It was just too much. He tore his attention from Julie long enough to discover that Dal Holcomb was no longer in the bar. He asked Gene where he was. Gene motioned toward the lobby and said, "There's a crap game going on out there, and I think you'll find Dal H. in the deep of it."

"I'll be back in a minute," Shaw said. "Why, the way my luck's running I should be in that game too. I'll wipe 'em out."

Dal was playing with two men, one whose nose was like Gene's but who was skinnier and looked sort of like a walking butcher knife. The other had the same cold eyes, very short legs, hardly any neck, and a square box—a yard across—for a torso.

In just fifteen minutes Shaw found that when the butcher knife picked up the dice they fairly screamed seven or eleven! In thirty minutes the rest of Shaw's three hundred was gone. Dal had already cashed five checks and was writing a sixth.

Shaw felt suddenly let down, and when he realized the bar was closing for the night he wanted to go to bed with Julie and be comforted. At the pace he was living he'd be an old man by his twenty-third birthday. He laughingly picked up his sketch, trying to show a jaunty, carefree attitude and trying to believe that the thirty-six hundred dollars he'd deposited would last.

Shaw didn't see the stiffening that took place in the anatomies of Gene and Julie, but when he took her hand to lead her to the doorway he felt the coldness of it, and when she told him good night, he knew it was good-bye.

He tossed his sketch pad in the pickup and instantly felt as lonely as a country schoolhouse in midsummer. He had learned more hard lessons in these two weeks in tiny Taos than he had in two years at the famed Chicago Art Institute.

4

Shaw and Zacharias Chacon, another new friend, were invited to lunch at La Cocina on the northwest side of Taos Plaza after meeting Dal Holcomb. Dal had received his check in the mail. Since there was no mail delivery, everyone met at the Taos Post Office two blocks north of the plaza.

Some people went there to visit when they got maybe three letters a year. However, most ordered various items from the Sears and Montgomery Ward catalogues for things that were unavailable in Taos, or often for things that were just available cheaper.

The three were seated in La Cocina by a waitress everyone knew and was fond of, Della Santistevan. Della, it seemed, had been a waitress in Taos forever but had stopped aging somewhere around thirty-five.

She was one Taos's most valued people, never forgetting a face or a joke or mistaking an order. Fast, personable, and efficient. She was a Taos treasure. Della had paid for a little home on Ranchitos Road and had three kids in high school and one in junior high by two different husbands. She clothed them, fed them, and did her best to raise them right. Della was an institution; although there were always one or two other waitresses in La Cocina, they always waited to give Della first shot at her chosen customers and tippers. Of course, everywhere Dal ate, drank, or simply visited, he was chosen because of his more than generous tips. Vern Matheny owned the place and did most of the cooking himself. His strongest point of gustatory delight was the chile rellenos that all three ordered. Many marveled that a gringo from an Amarillo, Texas, hamburger joint could make the best chile rellenos in northern New Mexico. Of course, in such a delightfully southwestern-decorated place, natural food naturally had more taste. Dal insisted they all have a scotch and water.

Shaw always felt a little guilty at such luxury when bargain wine was more to his and Zacharias's taste. However, after three or four drinks and the wondrous lightly crusted green chile rellenos plate, all economical thoughts were forgotten. The sopaipillas—the little, hollow pillowlike bread—that Matheny miraculously cooked with such thin outer crusts were filled with the customary honey and devoured as desert. This Taos confection wrapped up a meal of abundance—delicious abundance.

Now it was time for toasting everyone who had dined with the artist—Dal Holcomb knew that. The man of the big checks raised his glass and clinked it with Shaw's and Zacharias's, saying, "My friends, I will make this a better world, even if I have to kill everyone in it but me."

Shaw knew not where it came from, but he said, clinking glasses again, "What causes the wind to blow and the sun to burn is a question to some and an answer to others. It is always a wonder to me. I expect it is the same to a pissant."

Zacharias responded, "I knew that, but I just forgot to think it."

They all waited for Della to bring them their next drink, but they toasted confidently with their empty ones, which inspired Zacharias Chacon to expound, "Time has a very strong mind. It can fly in a wink, backward as fast as forward, up, down, sideways, at any speed, or become motionless; accelerate so fast it is invisible even to itself. Everything is controlled by time . . . even time itself. Time created thought and the word *forever*. Time can make a person famous or foolish. The highest mountain, a flat desert, or a planet burn and perish . . . in time."

Dal and Shaw were both amazed at the surprising words that flowed from Zacharias's mouth. How could it be? How?

Shaw knew there was no way he could even slightly approach that, so he said without thought, "My grandmother said that most of us use up life like a bottle of pills."

Now Dal Holcomb, the rich artist, was glowing as he thanked Della for the new glasses of scotch. They all clinked the now precious glasses full of the brown, and Dal wrapped up the toasting session with, "Here's to all that matters—art and love."

Zacharias said, in imitation of and in tribute to their drinking buddy, Indian Tony, "Dear brudder Dal, I say amen to that."

Shaw said, "I say amen to amen."

Vern Matheny came from the kitchen just at this moment to ask if the food had been alright. Of course he knew they would just love it. Being a good businessman as well as a fine chef, he'd really shown up to say hello to Dal Holcomb, the richest artist in Taos, or maybe the entire world at this glowing moment. The compliments from the three were as pleasing as a baby's laugh.

Young Shaw thought, *What a great evening in all the world, here in this chile joint in Taos, New Mexico.* Dal gave Della a big tip, and the three left to finish their evening in the Lucky Bar, where their best amigos would be hanging out and they could join them in consuming their first love, the liquid grape.

Shaw Spencer made the first toast there to the tune of an old Spanish love song on the jukebox. "You ain't nothing 'til you're something."

Indian Tony surprisingly joined in. After muttering part of it to himself, "Dear brudder knocked ol' Jolly Sandoval in the head with a full bottle of whiskey, broke it all to hell and wasted it."

It was almost unbelievable to Dal and Shaw, but Zacharias proved his mettle beyond a tinkle of doubt with a continuance of his time theory. "Time is measured geologically, by hourglass and clock mechanisms. There is daytime, nighttime, and mind time. Then there is time to be on time, but we don't always know about that. So . . . right next to it, unaware, we're about to enter a place we've never been, and the nothing time."

Since there were no clocks visible in the Lucky Bar for guidance, Zacharias shouted out, "See there, amigos, it is time for another drink," and he jumped up and did a dance so original that there was no way to name it.

All the friends in the Lucky Bar agreed, just as good friends would, that it was about time . . . And now came the Genius Time, better known as the Genius Hour, that unknown special moment around midnight when everyone knows they still have about two hours before the two o'clock closing time, and the wildest, most creative thoughts in all the world have reason to be expressed.

Dal Holcomb, the richest man in town—maybe in the world—said with the purest of joy, "I've got a great poem in my head—listen, amigos, listen with great care." They all did.

Hey, it's snowing.
Look, look at me
I can pee
Don't you see?
I wrote my name
It's all the same
But ain't it weird
I ran dry
Before the period.

To the loving amigos, Shakespeare wasn't even in it.

Zacharias raised a glass of the beautiful purple and committed a bit of thought. "Everything becomes round or a circle. Everything, finally. Try flying a square airplane, and the forces that be will knock all the corners off and crash to bits."

The Undertaker both listened and looked. He noticed the Lover staring at a pretty woman who was sitting at the bar surrounded by three men, all trying to win her attention. But she was staring beyond them and their talk at the Lover, who said, "Blessings, I do believe she almost smiled at me."

The Undertaker sympathized with his friend and said empathetically, "Those men don't even belong in the same cemetery with her."

The Spanish love songs played on. There was much smoke in the air from cigarettes and an occasional pipe. Shaw spoke now: "I resolve to make prayers for a big piñon and pine nut crop next fall so the squirrels can survive this squirrely world."

At the talk of squirrels Indian Tony ventured into the mixture of remembering. "Oh, my dear brudders, my dear pueblo friend, George One Horse, he got lost. Me and Augusta Big Tree, we go to find his tracks that center on this long line of bushes. Big Tree walk above the bushes. I walk below just like hunting deer. We throw rocks in the bushes to get George One Horse's attention. We walk and throw rocks. No George. No nothing. I just about give up. So, I throw the last rock—a big one. Then crash noises, and something falls out of the bushes rolling right next to my feet. I yell to Augusta Big Tree, Augusta, come down here. Poor Ol' George One Horse, he kill himself."

The jukebox stopped playing. Indian Tony was safely asleep in a booth. Zacharias and Shaw were last to leave after many thanks from the owner. All of the others had headed for their adobe homes and wives and kids and dogs and cats. It was a nice night with the lovely Taos moon shining in honor of all the sleeping workers, all the night watchmen, and all the wine lovers, the full moon's blue-green beauty making light to make shadows.

The moon had always been impartial. So it was this night, this little special time in history, in Taos, New Mexico. A dog barked just to let the world know he was there. The great sagebrush deserts surrounding the village softened like vast undulations of blue-green cotton, and coyotes voiced one another as far as hearing allowed. Taos, this special little place blessed by many moons, was for a few hours at peace.

5

ZACHARIAS CAST A WARM GLANCE toward the cheap wooden booth where the artist and the would-be artist abided, drinking and talking. He had already figured them for rich men. He also figured them to be kindhearted. Suddenly he felt this way himself.

They were celebrating the fact that Dal had just finished a commission for a Coca-Cola billboard. The check would be sizable, and they were spending it in advance. Dal, being eternally restless, had said, "Let's change the pace, Shaw, my boy. Let's go slumming."

So that's how they came to be in the Lucky Bar, although the slums of Taos were only two-thirds of a block long. Shaw continued to spend his bank account in the joyful manner of one who has unlimited funds.

Zacharias eased to the end of the bar and picked up a violin. Fingering the instrument tenderly, he played. It was a sad song of love and death, as most imported Mexican songs are. As life is.

Dal was suddenly reminded of old loves lost and gone, of parties that lived and died like theories, and he quickly, urgently, ordered drinks for the booth and Zacharias the musician. Shaw felt he should be affected, too, so he was.

"More, amigo! More!" Shaw yelled.

"Bravo! Viva!" Dal shouted.

Zacharias took his drink, smiled, and raised it in a toast to the booth. This was one of those lucky days. He could feel it, he could smell it, and for the final proof, he could taste it from the maroon-colored liquid in the unwashed glass. He relieved that glass of all responsibility in long, grateful swallows. And then he played again. It was his responsibility to play well now. His alone.

Although the music could not have carried much past the front glass of the Lucky Bar, the message had somehow penetrated the windows and adobes of the establishment and made contact up and down skid row. Inhabitants of the area began to gather.

There was Anna, the sometimes whore. She came in and sat at the bar, twisting around to look at the two artists so that her skirt pulled tight and revealed part of her smooth, brown thigh. Shaw looked and thought it was too bad that she wasn't cleaner. Dal Holcomb was so involved in the music he missed this tiny, not so subtle strip act.

Flavio Bernal, the Lover, came in. Looking around with his lover's eyes he immediately spotted Anna as well as an old woman in a back booth with an off-duty sheepherder. Since the women were not to his momentary use, he turned his attention to the two artists. So, this was why Zacharias was playing so much better than usual. Leave it to that Zacharias.

The Lover walked by Anna, rubbing her thigh and letting one finger sneak under the skirt where it was pulled tight. Having made his move and showed Anna he knew she was a female, he sat down at the bar and waited. The next best thing to a woman was a drink, and he knew that the latter would soon be coming. He was right. Shaw ordered drinks for everyone.

Dal motioned for Zacharias to come over to the booth. This is what Zacharias had been waiting for. Now he'd move in to consolidate his already enviable stature as a musician.

"Sit, sit," Dal said, gesturing his artist's hands grandly. "You play magnificently, amigo."

They were friends, alright, and the friendly liquid flowed and flowed as they talked of many things. Finally Zacharias could wait no longer. Touching the brim of his old gray hat tenderly and with compassion for its remaining faithfully in place, he said, "My friends, artists, and gentlemen. I'm sure you'll understand my position when I tell you this story of my struggle. You see, my amigos, I fell from a truck during the war and hurt my poor back. Now our good government owes me a vast sum of money for this injury received near the front lines while on duty—while serving my country. Today I am to receive a large check. Ten years of back compensation will amount to thousands of dollars. I can then fulfill my life's ambition . . ."

He leaned forward, waiting a moment to savor the expressions on his companions' faces. When he was satisfied with their impatient interest, he went on.

"You see, I learned to drive a bulldozer in the army. Later I worked up Twining Canyon on Bull of the Woods Mountain not far from here, on a copper mine. I scraped the overburden of soil from the ore deposit. But then the price of copper dropped in half, and I was again unemployed."

"Now you want to buy a bulldozer and go in business for yourself?" Shaw asked.

"That is right, friend Shaw. You have guessed it." The great dream lit Zacharias's red face. "Ah," he said, suddenly throwing both arms high toward the door, "here's Rosita now with my check!" Rosita walked straight to the booth without hesitation. "My daughter," Zacharias said proudly. "Rosita." Shaw examined her closely. There was a sensuousness about her that shouted, "Woman!" She gave Shaw a quick glance—just enough to let him know she'd looked a second time.

"Give me the check, Rosita. It is my turn to buy a drink."

"It did not come, Papa. Maybe tomorrow."

"Yes, tomorrow it will come," Zacharias said, with a slight raising of his shoulders.

"Good-bye, Papa." She nodded to Shaw. "Good-bye. It was nice to meet you." And before they could answer, she turned and swayed out of the place. At the door she glanced back at the Lover, who smiled and winked.

"Look," Zacharias said, and he pulled out the papers the government had sent him. Shaw and Dal read them.

"There's no doubt about it," Shaw said. "You are going to get a check—a big one."

"That is right," Zacharias agreed. "Tomorrow."

"I wouldn't count on that," Shaw said. "The government is slow, but certain."

Now Zacharias had the opening he had hoped for. "While I am waiting I need to go to Albuquerque and start bargaining on the great machine. It would take time and money but would save much in the long run. Especially time. And time is all we have. Is that not right, amigos?"

"Righto," Dal shouted, and he ordered more drinks for the house.

Anna was now dancing to the jukebox, swaying her plentiful hips like a Tahitian. Maybe not as gracefully, but with just as much meaning. The Lover watched her greedily. He didn't need Anna, but if one of the rich gringos didn't take her soon, he was obligated to all womankind to do so.

Zacharias continued, "If I could but find some gentleman who would invest with me, I would gladly give him ten percent of all my earnings from the machine."

Shaw looked at Anna's hind end swaying, swaying. "How much would it take?"

Zacharias felt his heart stop and then lurch ahead like a gutshot bear. How much did he dare ask for? He must have courage. "Oh, I think two hundred dollars would accomplish it."

Shaw could feel the drinks in his head. He could feel them in his thinking. He could almost feel the warm belly of Anna against his. She was looking at him now. The Lover sensed, in his sensitive soul, that a crucial moment was upon the Lucky Bar. He moved to Anna and danced her away into a corner in the back.

"Never mind," said Shaw, leaning out from the booth and looking for Anna. "It's a good investment for an artist. That's what artists need. More of them should put their money in something solid that will give returns. Isn't that right, Dal?"

"Yessh, thash right," said Dal. "Money is good, but what artists need most of all is guts, guts, guts! Musick! Musick! As the great philosopher, Aristotle, told the unhearing world long ago: All the world is family, and we are all related in our hearts."

So Zacharias played and played and felt good in his heart because others felt his music; his family at home, and his family here, listened and felt much.

In the interim the Lover, Anna, and a newcomer—Serapio Vargas, the Undertaker—had joined them at the booth. Extra stools were pulled up for those yet to arrive.

The Undertaker looked exactly like his name: except for a very fat face, he was skinny all over. He looked like a dead stick with a pumpkin stuck on its end. He dreamed of owning his own mortuary some day.

He loved death as the Lover did women. His favorite statement was, "Never fret, amigos, the same worms eat the rich as eat the poor." He attended every funeral, mass, and rosary, and he took as many jobs grave digging as his fragile body could manage. Whenever someone was critically injured, his finest hours were during the victim's last. The suspense of oncoming death elated him as opium does a doper, as a Rembrandt does an art student, as wine did Zacharias. Serapio loved wine, too, and was now pouring it down as fast as Shaw and Dal bought it. That was swift indeed. For this special night, in a special little place in a living world, for just this time, just these special moments—all was truly well. Happiness reined.

"My uncle Joseph is sick," Serapio beamed at each face at the table. "They say he has cancer of the stomach, and," he added, grinning across his bloated face—yellow like a rotten lemon—"cirrhosis of the liver as a bonus!" He rubbed his hands delightedly.

Shaw said, absentmindedly looking at him, "Poor fellow. Is there anything I can do to help?"

"Well," said the Undertaker, "if we could get him out of my Aunt Marie's sight, and take him on a week-long drinking binge, it might speed things up."

At this moment a little man stepped in from off the street. He was small and bent and lined like a three-year-old deer hide. But his eyes were big, soft, and black, with a depth that seemed to be looking beyond the galaxy. He wore old bib overalls that were sagging enough at the knees to afford room for six legs such as his.

Dal punched Shaw on the arm. "There's Patrociño Barela, the Woodcarver. He's a true original. He's famous. Barela is New Mexico's greatest artist. Recently one of his works sold to the Museum of Modern Art. The very first by a New Mexican."

Shaw stared at the one who qualified for such words of praise. It was obvious that he was also poor.

"Come here, Patrociño. Come and have a drink with us."

Dal motioned to a stool.

"Ho, it is Mr. Holcomb," said Patrociño, sitting down and motioning to the bartender, who knew already what brand of wine he wanted. "Tokay."

Patrociño's wood carvings of angels, devils, saints, love, lust, greed, and life were scattered in important collections all over the world. Many times he'd been written about in national and international magazines. But Patrociño didn't know he was an artist. Maybe that's why he was. He called himself a whittler, and he was amazed that anyone would pay for his carvings.

When Patrociño was a boy he had such a bad stutter that he seldom had the courage to talk, so instead he started whittling his feelings. He made a good trade with himself when he exchanged the rattle of his tongue for the action of his heart and hands in wood.

The one thing that impressed him about his own art was the fact he could satisfy his need for wine this way. Someone would always buy a carving from him. He carried them in a paper sack, and he felt guilty taking them out to show. He always asked for cash—always a dollar and a half, for he could buy an entire bottle of Tokay for that. The galleries sometimes would sell one for close to a hundred dollars, but this was rare.

Mr. Holt, up the street at the Taos Lodge, was his best customer. Why, he must have over two hundred of his works. Sometimes, if the piece was big enough and Barela was sober enough, Mr. Holt would give him three or four dollars for one. For years Mr. Holt waited for Patrociño to succumb to the evils of drink. He knew in his heart that if Patrociño died, the collection would grow greatly in cash value. But Patrociño kept on living—and even working. Now Mr. Holt himself was beginning to grow old, and though he sold lots of whiskey in his lodge, he didn't drink it. This was beginning to eat at him. What if, with all his clean living, Patrociño outlasted him? It was something to cause consternation in the covetous heart of the innkeeper.

So you see, even a man of great talent, of humility, of kindness and drunkenness causes a little sorrow in the world. He upset the schedule of cashed-in greed Mr. Holt had set for himself.

Patrociño welcomed the glass of wine set before him by the beaming bartender. It had been months since the Lucky Bar had done such a day of business. "To you, señors," he said, raising his glass of wine. "And to the Great Mystery in the Sky who made us all, and to us who have changed his wishes."

"Magnifico, Patrociño," said Dal, returning the gesture with his glass.

Patrociño pulled something out of a brown paper bag he took from the bosom of his overalls. Dal knew from past observation that he had a carving in the sack.

"Could we see it," Dal asked, his tongue having difficulty twisting the words out.

"Sure, señor," he replied, and his hands, those knobby, worn hands big enough for a man twice his size, lifted an archangel from the wrinkled paper bag as gently and tenderly as a mother would lift an injured offspring.

Shaw immediately fell in love with the angel and its primitive, exaggerated features. Its nose was one-fourth as long as its body. He picked it up, and even in this place of spilled drinks, open urinals, vomit-stained floors, and unwashed skin, he inhaled the clean, crisp smell of the mountain cedar from which the angel was carved.

"I want it. I want to buy it," he said. "How much?"

Patrociño raised his hands before him, shrugged his bent shoulders, and smiled from his deep, black eyes.

"Here, I'll give you all this," Shaw said, picking up a wad of bills from the table. "I won't count it if you won't."

Patrociño smiled and nodded his head yes. He ordered a drink for everyone there and a bottle for himself. This one day, this one moment of life, was complete for one man in the universe.

"You gave him too much, Shaw Boy," Dal said. "The man down the street steals them for one-fifth as much."

Shaw said, "There is no such thing as too much for something as rare as this. Besides, I'm not the man down the street."

Anna was sitting across from Shaw now, and he could feel her leg rubbing up against him. The Lover sat next to her, caressing the upper portion of that same leg, feeling a deep obligation to live up to his name at all times.

Dal looked at Anna and said, "What a head. What structure. Shaw, you should paint this girl."

Shaw hadn't thought about that. Now he studied Anna. It was true her face was big, but it did have a fine structure. The cheeks pushed up like crab apples, and the mouth was big, full of white teeth, and ringed with heavy, almost surplus lips. The eyes were shaped and sized like hens' eggs and seemed made of wet shadows. Her hair was black and smelled like it had been washed over three weeks ago and sprayed with low-cost perfume every day since. He could smell her otherwise, the perspiration that ran down under strong arms and beaded on her forehead when she danced the Tahitian alone. Her breasts were round. Shaw figured it would take both his hands to cover them. Her waist angled in nicely above buttocks the size of half-bushel baskets.

Anna thought of herself as a peddler—a peddler of apples. All the apples came in the basket below her stomach. She sold one here, one another place. The basket never went empty, so once in a while—very rare—she would give a few away. And that's what she felt like doing right now.

She smiled at Shaw, stretched backward, and clasped one of his legs between the two of hers. She could afford to feel generous. Shaw had been sending her to play the jukebox all night. Each time he'd handed her a bill of unknown denomination. She'd kept all the change. It amounted to something between eighteen and twenty dollars. Tomorrow she would go to Safeway and buy enough food to last her and her widowed mother for a month. She would get her arthritic mother two jars of snuff to repay her for the times of continued love and care while Anna peddled her apples.

In the Lucky Bar tonight there was much happiness among the imbibers. The drinks were unlimited.

The Lover left the table and went to the bar, where two girls sat. He ordered them drinks and told the bartender his friend Shaw would take care of it. He told the two girls about his rich artist friend and how he could always get anything he needed from him. He whispered other things in their ears, too. Soon, after three drinks so generously bought by the Lover via Shaw Spencer, he left with a girl on each arm. He walked out knowing the others stared in wonderment. He didn't dare look back to let them know he cared so very much about his reputation.

The Undertaker was drinking slowly now. His fat head was wobbling on his skinny neck. He was imagining himself as a true, terribly efficient undertaker, with his own establishment during a time of pestilence and plague, with bodies everywhere and hearses pulling in and out, disposing of one corpse and loading another in endless procession. He was in charge of embalming, of makeup, of all arrangements, and it was he who said to the bereaved, "Fear not, weep not, dear ones, for you shall soon join the grieved and departed."

Zacharias, being a very sensitive man, must have picked up some of the Undertaker's thoughts, for he said with the greatest of generosity, "Dear Serapio, when I get the check, my pardner Shaw and I shall buy you a complete funeral. Flowers by the ton, a black hearse as long as this bar, and mourners from the whole county. It will be up to you to furnish the body."

"Zacharias, you are a true friend. For such a gesture I would truly give my own body if necessary."

Anna now had Shaw's hand and was tickling his palm. Dal was drinking silently, listening, when Matias, the Fighter, stumbled up, fell against the table, and spilled some drinks. He stood weaving, trying to brace himself for the blow that was sure to come. It didn't. Everyone there liked him and understood without having to ask.

When the blows failed to materialize, Matias stood in his tracks and dreamed. He dreamed of his little mama, of his small brothers and sisters, and of his big fat daddy who had eaten most of the food and beat them all with his fat fists and who finally left one night never to return. Matias had always wanted to find his fat daddy of a deserter and repay him. But, of course, he never would. Now the brothers and sisters were grown and gone away, and his mother was so old she couldn't remember when she was born.

Matias had once been a Golden Gloves Champion, and a very handsome one. He loved to fight. Now there was just one drawback to this—it had been years since he could throw a punch hard enough to bend bamboo. He seldom ate, this Matias. He just drank and dreamed. His once handsome face was scarred and unrecognizable. His eyes were no longer white around the edges but a reddish brown, so it was hard to tell when his eyeballs turned in their sockets. He'd absorbed innumerable beatings. In this way he was tough, but his brain had shifted around in his head so that round things now appeared square to him and distance and time were interwoven in a world made of ether and elements of ghosts.

He stumbled across the barroom floor boxing at shadows. The Undertaker followed him with sympathetic but greedy eyes. If he was lucky, someone would beat Matias to death the day Zacharias got his great check. Now wouldn't that be something? He would get to plant his dear old friend. He drained the wine glass dry and breathed the fumes in total anticipation. How lucky for Matias to have a friend so dedicated. He, Serapio, would make it a thing of sad beauty.

Dal was about to go to sleep sitting up. Shaw pulled him to his feet and motioned for Anna to come with them. They shook hands with everyone about two dozen times before they could get out of the bar. One thing they had here was friends, the friendliest of friends.

Dal had wanted to go slumming, but the slum had just about done him in.

Anna followed Shaw as he loaded Dal into the convertible. Dal was too drunk to drive, so they left him to sleep it off. Besides, Shaw was in a hurry to get home and paint a portrait of Anna before the inspiration was gone. First he loved her as she expected, even though he was full of drink. Then he put his clothes back on. It would embarrass him to paint in the nude. Some crude person might enter without knocking.

The next day Shaw put the last brush stroke on the canvas, stepped back, and let out a yell. He'd done it, a picture of Anna, and it was good. He knew it was good—good for an amateur like him, that is—and yet he needed someone else to tell him so. He took the wet painting and drove to the adobe compound in Talpa where Dal lived.

He found him sitting on the patio, absorbing the mountain sun that pulled the remaining alcohol from his body. Dal got up and walked toward the pickup before it came to a full stop. He saw the canvas leaned back against the seat and knew what was coming.

As they took the picture over to the shade of the porch and looked, Shaw felt his hands perspiring and his heart beating like a trapped quail's.

Dal squinted his eyes, adjusted his horn-rimmed glasses, and moved back and forth. Would he never comment? It had been hours since he'd first looked, days, eternities, Shaw thought.

"It's good, Shaw my Boy. It's really good."

The elation of a successful creation surged through Shaw, but he couldn't say much.

"Would you like some coffee?"

"Man, I sure would," he said. Dal carried the painting into the studio with them and set it on his empty easel. Then he went to the kitchen to put the coffee on. They sat where they could both look at the picture.

"She looks happy, that girl. You must have made her happy just before you painted this, Shaw. No one can fake that look on a face. You've painted a woman, a she-woman. A female from out of the apple garden."

"I was lucky."

"Yeah, that's right. It takes luck to get a painting that speaks. This is the only criterion for a successful painting: if it projects beyond the frame. What's the important thing in this picture to me, beyond the luck, is the feeling you had for the woman, or even more, it seems to me, for another human being. That's damned crucial. If you hate, it shows. If you love, it shows. But if you do neither, you're dead."

"I felt it all right," said Shaw, embarrassed and thrilled at the same time.

Dal Holcomb brought out the coffee and spoke as he handed the dark liquid to Shaw. "You know, if I've learned anything at all in this little worthless life of mine, it's this. Aside from all the obvious talents of humankind, we have only two that dominate. The power to create and the power to destroy. I think you're a potential creator of much worth."

"Well, I don't know what to say."

"Don't! Just work!"

6

HIS WORK BURST WITH CRUDE FORCE—the force of life itself in all its varied movements, rhythms, and colors. He sought subjects of deep feeling and mood, ethereal and earthy.

He painted all day and into the night now. He painted the adobe buildings and winding burro streets of Taos. He painted the blanketed, dignified Indians, the children of the alleys, and the old Spanish men. To go a step further, he glued a huge canvas on the ceiling of his own adobe house that was to be his first great work. He built a movable board platform so he could lie on his back and paint like Michelangelo. It was an excruciating position to paint from, but he had to know if his veins carried the talent and the guts of the great. How else to gain the knowledge? And then he needed to go to the earth, and so he drove into the desert.

He drove now toward the new Long John Dunn Bridge that spanned the dark, a seven-hundred-foot gash made by the Rio Grande River, and wound his way up to the top and out into the sagebrush of the desert.

He parked and listened and felt. A great silence surrounded him. He felt the stillness as a speck, the vastness as a home, and the loneliness as a blessing. Suddenly the desert moved before his eyes and bulged up into mountains, and then the mountains sank into the desert like a ship into the sea. Then they returned like a newborn island. The sky flapped its wings and smiled. The sun cooled a moment and sent a flare five hundred thousand miles high to lick at the universe with a tongue of fire. All was movement. He looked again into the Sangre de Cristos, where they mashed the sky asunder, and he wanted to go there too.

In the weeks that followed, his work grew in quality and quantity until he had enough canvases for his own one-man show. Dal gave a party to announce and celebrate this fact.

At this party Shaw, the painter, the would-be artist, met Stella, the girl, his first real romance since high school. It began suddenly, flared briefly, and then disappeared like the wine from Zacharias's glass.

Stella, her mother, and her father—a moneylender from Kansas City—were staying at the Sagebrush Inn. They came to Taos every summer for a two-week vacation. Her parents were the usual combination of affability and coldness that was exuded by most moneylenders. He didn't have the dignity of being a banker, and the lives he dealt in were for small stakes. LOANS UP TO A THOUSAND DOLLARS ON YOUR SIGNATURE graced the sign on his establishment. And by law there should have been this added: BESIDES THE VAST INTEREST CHARGED, I WANT THREE AND ONE-HALF PINTS OF YOUR BLOOD QUARTERLY.

The well-tanned, graying man of money and his well-dressed, bleached-blonde wife with her fixed smile both congratulated Shaw on his exhibit and mentioned having heard nice things about him from Mr. Holcomb. It was obvious that Dal spoke to them from the position of over forty thousand a year; the national reproductions of his works most certainly made him a voice to be heard.

Shaw ignored them, sensing they were saying this for Dal's benefit, not his. He gave all his attention to their daughter.

She'd been out of college two years, and that's all he knew about her except that she was small and willowy with sultry, planned movements. Her hair was long and brown and surrounded a model's face with eyes like semi-whore Anna's. Her mouth twisted this way and that around a perfect set of teeth.

"I'm Stella."

"I'm Shaw. You want a drink?"

She looked at him and, just to be different, said, "No."

"You don't drink?"

"Of course I drink. It's just that I'm tired of these parties. It doesn't matter where they give them, in Taos, Beverly Hills, or Kansas City, they're all the same."

"Come on, then. I'll take you to my studio. Maybe that'll be different."

"I think I might like that," she said, and she picked up a yellow stole, slung it insolently over her shoulder, and took his arm. They left.

That's how it started. She liked his paintings, and he showed her the huge canvas ceiling where the charcoal sketch was only now taking some shape. And he told her of his artistic dreams. At first she seemed interested, then bored. Then interested again.

He had that feeling a young man gets when he loses his virginity. He felt the flow of love, even if he didn't know what love was. He also felt like he was still in high school, and he wondered if he still looked like it.

He touched her, and they talked on and on of life and art and many profound things that neither one knew very much about. They would both learn, but on different paths.

Before the evening was over, Shaw actually believed he would get her for himself before her two-week stay was up. He'd decided to keep her here in Taos regardless of her father's decision. But, of course, Shaw didn't know about the power and smallness of Jesus H. Money yet. That came shortly after.

He took her to all the galleries, and they went out around town at night, and then he knew he must make his move if he was to get Stella. Wherever they went now, her small, warm hand was in his or her head was bent over, touching his shoulder. He just knew she was his forever, but he decided to use nature to absolutely cinch it. He invited her for a walk in the woods.

"It's a rough climb," he told her, "so wear Levis."

The two young things drove into the mountains up Twining Canyon. The sun was climbing from its hiding place toward the edge of the world.

"Father was awfully put out with me," she said, "for going with you today."

"Why?"

"I've told you before. He wants me to marry into the company. He's afraid you'll seduce me and take me away from his little green-paper world." She twisted her head and smiled at him almost wickedly.

By God, Shaw thought to himself, *this girl's going to get it before the day's over, and Shaw the artist is going to give it to her. Papa or no Papa, she won't leave after today.*

He turned the pickup into a side canyon. About a month ago he'd sketched a picture up this canyon, and he remembered what a hell of a climb it was. He wanted to see if this girl was tough. She'd have to be tough to be an artist's woman.

He drove up the road until it turned into a game trail. Two large, fallen trees blocked the pickup. The sun was just rising, announcing itself and seeming to fill the world like the star of a TV series holding court in a small bar.

As they got out, Shaw said, "Just follow me, honey."

The underbrush along the dim, winding trail was wet and heavy with dew. In a very few minutes their pants were soaked through above the knees. Walking was difficult and uncomfortable. It was cold. They circled around, over and under fallen spruce and aspen limbs. Stella came on, much to Shaw's surprise and pleasure.

Finally the sun crept above the protruding mountains. Shaw stopped to give Stella a rest. She started to sit down.

"No, not yet," he said. "It's still too cold. You'll get so stiff you can't walk."

Shaw eased over to the South Fork Creek. The graveled bottom was clearly visible where the crystal-green water slowed or pooled. He looked until his eyes adjusted to the coloration, and he could see seven or eight trout. One was very large. He motioned, signaling silence, for her to come see.

"Look," he whispered. "Just left of that log."

She looked intently. Then she shook her head in puzzlement. All of a sudden she squealed and clapped her hands. "Shaw! Fish!" At her movement all the fish darted out of sight. "Oh, I'm sorry," she said. "I frightened them."

"It doesn't matter. We'll find some more," he said, walking upstream to another pond.

"There! There!" she said excitedly, but softly. "See, right there."

He followed her pointing hand to three trout facing upstream, almost motionless. He had a hell of a time keeping her moving. For the next half mile all she wanted to do was look for fish.

Suddenly a big buck and three does dashed across a pond and stopped in a clearing of aspens a short distance away. They froze, and so did the hikers. The animals' bodies were aimed toward the timber, but each head was arched back in the direction of the humans. The sun beamed through the leaves, reflecting lights here and there on the great rack of antlers. The does stood waiting for the buck to signal or move. Shaw and Stella held their breath. As they exhaled, the buck whirled and the does went with him in absolute unison, disappearing into the timber.

Stella watched awhile silently. "So beautiful," she said in a half whisper, "so pure and beautiful."

Shaw looked at her and thought how beautiful she was, but he was going to have to hold off on his judgment of her purity.

The climb was getting steeper, and even in this high altitude, with the cold, wet undergrowth, they were perspiring.

A flock of mountain grouse whizzed from one growth of thick trees to another on the opposite side of the creek. Shaw called attention to a bear track in the mud along the bank.

"They look like human feet," Stella said.

The sun had now nearly reached its zenith. As it began to arc to the south, the spruce developed a pure light-blue haze under their limbs, and where the sun struck them directly they turned from green to glowing yellow.

Shaw was becoming very tired himself. He was elated to see that Stella was still following, although he figured it must take a lot of courage now for her to keep going. He felt a momentary twinge of guilt and slowed for her. It did no good; she just slowed with him, staying the same four or five steps behind.

Then they burst into the clearing where he'd done his sketching. The creek made a horseshoe here, outlining the small, quiet meadow. Up ahead the barren brown rock above timberline contrasted with the verdant greens below. This he'd painted back in his little studio. The grass lay about, thick, lush. Up ahead the aspens had started turning yellow.

It looked as if a giant had strolled across the land carrying a huge ladle of melted gold and had here and there spilled some on the dark forest.

They stopped by a pine tree of extreme size and sat in the sun for a smoke and to catch their breaths.

Shaw said, "This is what I painted."

"I remember it in your studio. I can't imagine you having the strength to paint after that climb."

That was the nearest she came to complaining about it. She'd passed the test, Shaw thought. Now it was up to him.

The warm sun relaxed their muscles, and they dozed side by side. Shaw awakened a little while later, stood up, and looked down at the girl. She was asleep, breathing deeply, steadily. Her shirt tail was out, and the top of her jeans was undone. He could see the whiteness of the skin on her stomach and the top of her silk panties. A sudden desire grasped him. His legs weakened, and he knelt beside her and stretched out full-length.

She was warm. He kissed her and tasted her breath, which came directly out of her mouth and into his. She stirred a little, and he put her arms around his back without saying a word. Then it was more than they could bear, and they made love in a remote canyon high in the mountains, with the creek's swift murmur blending with that of their blood. A tiny breeze caressed the grass around them, and the warmth of the sun bestowed its blessings upon Shaw's back.

A long while later they sat up.

Shaw said, "I want you. Do you understand? I want you for always."

She looked closely into his eyes, touched him on the temples with the fingertips of both her hands, then jumped up quickly and ran to the creek, dropping her clothing all in a pile on the bank.

Shaw got up and ran after her, yelling, "You'll freeze in that water!"

She paid no attention to him. She splashed herself all over. There was a large fallen log across the creek. Shaw crawled out on the log, laid flat on his belly, and watched her. She was shivering as she walked upstream toward the log. She stopped in a whirlpool and looked at the water around her.

The sun caught in the ripples and reflected around her navel and radiated out like the shattered surface on a still, clear pond. The sun gleamed through her hair, which looked more bronze than brown. Her dark, mystical eyes caught images of the creek, and they seemed kin. The grace of her, the utter beauty of her whole being at this moment, the way her soul seemed to have welded with her surroundings hypnotized Shaw. Her nakedness seemed as pure as the air around them. Shaw didn't want to paint her, but he achingly wanted her, and forever and ever, he thought.

The walk back down was slow and even restful in spite of being hard going. By the time they reached the pickup, the canyon had turned dark, but the sky above was still shot with color.

Stella grabbed him and said, "Thanks, Shaw. Thanks for bringing me here."

Shaw could say nothing. He just held her body until the sky turned violet.

That's the way it ended. Her parents loaded her up and took her back to Kansas City the next morning. Shaw couldn't believe that he would never hear from her again. His heart ached for her. His head ached for her. Even his toes ached for her. But gradually it lessened until it was no more.

Dal told him casually one evening, "Remember that girl Stella?"

"Yeah."

"I just got a wedding announcement from her."

"That's nice." And Shaw thought of what a good painting and an even better piece of tail he'd received from the mountain glade last fall. Young Shaw was changing swiftly, like a combat soldier surviving his first full day of bloody battle.

7

"VIVA LA FIESTA," said Indian Tony.

"Happy fiesta is right," said Zacharias.

"It's a fine day," said Juandias, the Woodhauler, looking up at the clear sky. "But in just a month now it'll be cold enough to sell wood." And, of course, he went about it in his own way. This was how he made his living. He took wood from land that was not his, and then he sold it at twice the usual price.

He would say, "Like some good piñon wood, mister?" He knew the words "good piñon" were magic to the newcomers of Taos. He remembered all faces, so it was no problem to pick out the new arrivals each year. "Come, let me show you this fine wood. It's a big bargain for only five dollars." The back of the pickup would indeed appear to be full. This was but another of life's many illusions, for the bottom of the truck bed was half full of small pieces of bark and tiny broken limbs. This part of the load remained in place. Each of his customers paid for this wood without receiving it. No one questioned him about it, although he'd seen a few strange expressions, and he rarely ever made a second sale to that customer. Sometimes just under the top layer of piñon were large chunks of pine that weren't nearly as good for fireplaces but were so much easier for him to get. Well, it was one way of making a living.

During his years as a negotiator, Juandias had learned the value of surprise. For instance, this very morning he had dashed from his old truck to the door of a gringo's house with a dozen eggs in a basket. He knocked urgently. A man came to the door smoking a pipe and holding a newspaper. This was good, Juandias thought; he's not well awake yet.

"Dear sir," he said with the utmost urgency in his anxious voice, "I

46

have here one dozen eggs I gathered in a great hurry. My wife is very sick. I must get medicine quick. She is sick as a woman gets who has the baby early. Understand, dear sir?"

"Well . . . I . . . uh . . ."

"Dear sir, could you let me have three dollars in a big hurry. I'll bring six dozen eggs right back. I must have medicine for mama and the early baby." Juandias knew this last bit got them in their weak spot, and at this very moment Juandias could feel the three dollars wadded up in his pocket. It was a bounteous sum to have for fiesta, especially this early in the morning. Why, it was an hour before the parade started. He was secure for the day. He was happy. All this for one dozen eggs, which his large family would have eaten in only one day. And the man with the pipe and paper would have something to occupy his mind. He could wonder from now on when Juandias would show up with the six dozen eggs.

Yes, it was a good day, and if his friends Indian Tony and Zacharias were pleasant he would let them share in his bounty. It went against his grain to cut Tony in on the results of his morning's work, but then he had to remember the past times that Tony had shared his bottle of delight, as well as times in the future when he might. You never knew about these Indians. They could possibly get rich from the government some day. He'd heard about the Utes in Utah getting millions of dollars and the Navajos becoming wealthy on oil and uranium. A careful man thought of these things.

Zacharias had learned much from the Native Americans. But for now he studied Juandias intently. Was that particular tilt to his greasy baseball cap indicative of something? Was the fact that he had now been in the same spot for over ten minutes of importance? He decided it was. This is the longest he could ever remember Juandias standing in one place without a bottle or a glass of wine. Something was definitely churning.

"Juandias, you're looking well. How's the family? The niños?"

"They're healthy and well fed," Juandias said lightly. "And my own fine appearance is due to the success of my woodhauling business."

"This early in the year?"

"No, I have prospects for later. My nephews have already hauled a winter's supply for the back of my truck. And the Indians have prophesied a bad winter. Is that not so, Tony?"

Indian Tony wrapped his blanket around his shoulders a little tighter and said, "I sure of that, dear brudder."

"Of course, I have to share the profits with my nephews, but then they both left for California last week, so I won't have to pay until spring or maybe later."

"How are your chickens?"

"Oh, they still lay. The wife has sorted out sunflower seed all fall, and I have two sacks of corn that I found lying by the highway. They're in good shape for the winter. And, too, I hear that eggs are going up. Way up."

"How could they get any higher?" asked Zacharias, whose family had been without eggs for years.

"I heard this morning that a dozen eggs brought three dollars."

"Three dollars? What kind were they?"

Juandias could contain himself no longer. He pulled the three dollars from his pocket and stuck them before Zacharias's unbelieving eyes.

Zacharias stood up and said admiringly, "My friend, you've done it again." He invented a dance, not knowing or caring what it was. He whirled, he jigged, he tapped, and he said, "Greek."

Tony licked his lips, pulled his blanket in every direction, and said, "Dear brudder."

Juandias made his purchase, and soon the fiesta was a fiesta.

People were gathering around the plaza now, waiting for the parade. Every available parking space was filled for blocks in all directions. Tourists were loading and adjusting cameras. Everyone was crowding forward, holding children up to see the colorful pageantry. The dominant subject of the procession was Taos history. Famous personages such as Governor Bent and Kit Carson were presented, along with many horseback riders dressed like conquistadors, trappers, and priests. The Indians, representing themselves, danced around the plaza with their feathers flashing like little rainbows, and bells on their ankles blended with the chants and drums.

Then came the children's parade. They carried dogs and cats and led goats and sheep, calves and chickens. They were painted and dressed like clowns, cowboys, spacemen, and mountain men, and some of the little girls were dressed for a miniature Folies Bergère. Later they would stand in line to ride *tiovivo*, the ancient, hand-cranked merry-go-round.

Everyone, touched for a moment by the colorful past, clapped and smiled. Zacharias felt the music of the school band go down his throat and into his blood with a large swallow of his friend's wine. Indian Tony listened to his "brudders" dancing and playing for the pleasure of the crowd.

They sat, the three of them, on the Resting Place and listened and heard and felt. There was no need for them to leave their place of comfort and pleasure to fight the masses from the plaza. They had seen it all in the past, and it was always about the same to one who lived there. For sure it was enjoyed more from a distance by these three, who now became four with the arrival of Matias the Fighter.

He stood, weaving slightly. "Viva la fiesta," he said, and he waited.

The bottle went around, and then Zacharias handed it to the Fighter. He took it in a skinned hand, which he held so that all could see the damage done to his knuckles by the mighty blow he'd struck only the day before.

He said, "Three of them. Big ones! Punks! Big ones!" and pointed to his half-closed eyes, his purplish, swelled lips, and his skinned nose. This nose never healed anymore. It had been hit so hard and so often it had now taken it upon itself to remain on the permanent injury list. Why bother to heal? It would be a waste time on this fist-battered face.

The Fighter tilted the bottle with his skinned knuckles prominently displayed. Actually, this injury had occurred when he struck at a ten-year-old boy who was standing many yards away. Not only was Matias's judgment of distance off, but his accuracy was decidedly out of order. Instead of the boy, he had hit the side of the Home Food Store, but nevertheless he felt a delicious thrill run up his arm from the bleeding hand. He thought for a moment he'd found and struck his big, fat, deserting, wife-beating daddy. He'd felt elated all night, telling his old, old mother that they could probably get the welfare check doubled now that he'd avenged her desertion. This morning, however, he wasn't so sure. Maybe he'd just imagined it all. He'd asked several people if they had seen his father. No one had.

"What does your father look like?" one tourist had asked.

"He's fat, and he has a broken jawbone," said the Fighter, going into the crouch with his fists moving up weakly. At this thought he tipped the bottle up again, and it took both Zacharias and Indian Tony to get it down before it was empty. The Fighter had considerable strength when gripping a bottle.

They all three fell to the ground in a tangle. At last Tony came up with the bottle. It was the third one, in fact, that had been purchased with the high-priced egg money. Indian Tony was now in the most favorable position he could imagine. He was sitting, almost lying down, and he had to his lips a bottle that he'd won in a fair struggle.

In a little while most of the crowd from the plaza would go to the Indian Pueblo to watch the pig races, the greased pole climb, more dancing, and all the other things the Indians do to celebrate San Geronimo Fiesta. Indian Tony would miss the doin's.

Other friends gathered around the Resting Place, and soon the three dollars was gone. It really didn't matter much on fiesta, because there would be many drunks around the plaza, and there would be free drinks in abundance for those with the courage or the cunning to make the right approach.

They all gradually sauntered away, leaving Indian Tony alone to guard the Resting Place. He didn't mind. He was ahead of them all. He dreamed.

The indigenous people of the pueblo had been on guard for nearly a thousand years.

8 THE FIESTA WENT ON FOR TWO DAYS, and then it was
over. The Resting Place was full of woe. Each head felt like many, and
the trembles afflicted all. But none complained. That would have been
a dishonor among the winos. Only alcoholics, hooked on hard brown
whiskey, and those who took the ladies' drink—known as *Martinez* or
some such—complained.

Zacharias sat and talked to the Lover. "I must tell you something,"
Zacharias began.

"I feel from your voice it'll not make me leap and bound with joy."

"That is up to you, my son."

"Is it about Rosita?"

"Si, amigo, you have guessed it."

"Is she going to get married?"

"That's right," said Zacharias, and for once he was so carried away
that he actually took his old gray hat from his head and scratched at
his thin hair.

"May I ask who the lucky man will be?"

"That is a privilege you most certainly deserve, and out of my respect
for your taking my daughter's one prize, her virginity, from her, I will
go ahead and relieve you of the burden of asking."

The Lover rose up as if to run from the Resting Place. "Hold it right
there, amigo, and listen to my words!" The Lover pointed at himself,
silently asking a question with his handsome but frightened eyes.

"AYAAA. You, Flavio Bernal, the lover of Taos women, the lover of all
women, will now have a chance to concentrate your talents and confine
them to one. Just one! Do you hear?"

The Lover looked behind him. He was sure someone was about to stab him in the back with a broken bottle. He knew that Zacharias only used this type of speech when he had a definite point to make. There was a coldness about his being that made him glance all around like a wild fox in a living room. His mouth moved, but no sound emerged other than a sort of moan.

"She is with baby. Your baby, my dear son-in-law."

The Lover sat back down. The trembling continued. At last his voice returned.

"Are you sure, Zacharias? She's been out with a dozen men. Why, just last night at the fiesta, I saw her necking with a farmer from Peñasco. Why must I take the blame?"

"It does not matter, my son-in-law. Women know about these things. You are chosen. So you see, it does not matter."

The Lover saw.

"When?"

"As you like, but by the end of the year. I realize you'll have much explaining to do around town."

"Yes. Much."

At that moment the Iron One came into view. He moved a few feet and then stopped, holding himself up with his wooden stick. He never raised his feet but shuffled them three or four steps at a time, stopped, and then moved on again, over and over. Some said he was ninety-five years old. Others said he was over a hundred. There was no doubt about his being ancient.

Zacharias stood and held himself erect for a moment in respect. Even the Lover forgot his troubles momentarily. The Undertaker licked his lips as Indian Tony would at the sight of a new bottle of wine.

Out of respect Serapio spoke under his breath. "Ah, Iron One, even you shall go the way of all mortals. I shall see you to the final home, back to the one great womb. I shall dig your grave before this winter is over. Last winter you could take five steps without stopping, now two of those have been erased from your abilities. You will soon be done, and then the Iron One will become the Rusty One and then dirt."

The Iron One had been old and drunk, wasted, half blind and two-thirds deaf when all those who stood and watched were either still in their father's crotch or were tiny children. He had on one occasion, years before, consumed three and a half bottles of red wine in three hours and still walked home—and all this without food. No one had ever done it since.

He drank for fifty years or more like this. Then he understood he was different, that the wine would not kill him, so he tired of it and quit. He was a walking legend. Every day at his advanced age he walked to the plaza and back home. Two twisting blocks, uphill, downhill, with his five—and now three—steps at a time. He had to feel his way with the stick, and the loudest of noises was only the dullest of sounds. Maybe not even a sound, more of a vibration than anything else, and yet he stood upright in the world and moved. All of them sensed his glory and his supremacy, and they spoke of him in reverent tones. All, that is, except the Undertaker, who would only worship him when he was forever motionless. The Iron One's name was Hans Paap. He painted around the world, but his paintings sold for such low prices that he barely made enough to exist. Never enough for a living.

The Undertaker carefully observed, "Gravity is collapsing his bones and pulling his head toward the blessed earth." He mused a brief moment and then went on. "Gravity is the only absolute fact. The only one."

Zacharias enjoined, "No, amigo, no. A man can't have a baby, but the Great Mystery in the Sky put teats on him just in case he did."

Indian Tony explained this wisdom, nodding toward Zacharias, "He went to collich."

Zacharias had on occasion been using his elevated thoughts and speech. He mused that he must be more careful about that. Señor Buick had given him much stature, but he must be more careful about his speech so the unofficial members of the Grape Club would better understand him.

The Iron One disappeared at long last down the street. The others breathed again and sat on the rail and took up their own thoughts.

Some of the audacity and courage that gave him his name had returned to the Lover. The Iron One had inspired him. Wasn't he just as great with his own capacities? True, he was not such a drinker, but that was not all there was in the world. A great deal to be sure, but not all.

"I'll agree to marry your daughter, Zacharias, my father-in-law, even though I'm innocent. However, I'll not vouch for my faithfulness until I'm at least as old as you."

"That'll be all right. I'm not going to ask the world of you. I'm not so old. I realize one can't just quit like that." He snapped his fingers. "The shock to your delicate system would be too much. But I must insist that you keep your word, and each year make it one less woman until you've completely broken the habit—except for Rosita, of course."

"Oh, with her I'm sure it'll increase. You'll soon be a grandfather many times."

"I've always wanted that. Here comes Rosita now with my check."

The Lover got up and moved hastily into the liquor store even though his pockets were empty.

Rosita came up with her soft womanly movements in evidence.

"Where did Flavio go?" she asked possessively.

"He had to talk business with someone. He'll be right back."

"Did you speak to him?"

"Yes, it is all set."

"Ah, Papa," she said, and she threw her arms around him and squeezed him hard with her face in his chest.

"The check?" he said, feeling embarrassed in front of his friends.

"It didn't come today, Papa. Perhaps tomorrow."

"Yes, tomorrow," he said, disengaging himself, looking, hoping he would see the bright-orange sweater of his pardner, Shaw Spencer, walking up. "Look, Rosita, I must tell you something. We are getting a new car. A Buick."

"A new one?"

"Only twelve years old. It's green."

"Where is it?" she asked, holding her arms across breasts that would soon fill with milk.

"In the garage for a final tune-up. We can have it for tomorrow. Now, go home and break the news to Mama, and tell her we'll go for a long ride tomorrow."

"Where did you get the money, Papa? Did the check come without my knowing?"

"No, my pardner, Mr. Spencer, bought it for me. I haven't yet told him. I feel it would be better to surprise him at a later date with the good news."

"He must be a kind man," Rosita said, "but I hear he is an idiot who paints on ceilings."

"He knows his business."

"But Papa, no one wants to lie on their back and look at a painting."

Flavio, the Lover, came up and said, "Don't worry, Rosita. Anna will be his whole audience. She does most of her business on her back anyway."

Zacharias Chacon stood up majestically, wrathfully. "Go," he said. "Get away from me, both of you. Never speak of my friend like that again." He turned and walked away. The two stood and stared silently at the stiffness of his back.

Zacharias was having a rare bountiful day with his finances. He had repaired the Guzman's backyard door by resetting a hinge so it would close without showing. And he had mowed the artist Zachendorf's lawn and repaired the front gate. He had $3.75 to share. Seventy-five cents for himself, and three dollars for Mama.

9

THEY RAN A MODEST NOTICE in the *Taos News* about Shaw
Spencer's first one-man show at the Sagebrush Inn. Dal helped him
make all the preparations. This included a huge bowl of punch spiked
with hundred-proof vodka and, of course, hanging the pictures in the
vast lobby.

The show opened on a Saturday afternoon in November with Dal
already full of punch, feeling, somehow, that it was a show of his own
work as well as his protégé's. For a while it didn't seem as if anyone
would come, but the punch will always get them out. There were a few
hotel guests looking at the paintings with a casual interest, trying to act
like they knew what they were seeing, while others just hurried around
and out, rushing by before someone could ask what they thought. This
would never do!

Then they started coming all at once. Local artists of all kinds: the
old and settled, the young, the curious, the critical, and those on the
fringes who were always present to absorb the punch, small talk, and
whatever little glory they could gather from association.

At first they all took punch and scattered out among the pictures
in little groups. An occasional loner really studied the work, or at least
appeared to.

Shaw was nervous. He constantly returned to the punch bowl and
lit cigarettes as fast as he could. Dal had already told him to ignore the
opinions of those present because he would hear only good to his face.
He added that the only true way to tell if the show was a success was
to observe the number of people who remained after the punch was
gone. That wouldn't be long.

A tall man and a short man, both married to rich women, and both of whom now painted at their leisure and socialized their work into prominence, nodded to him on their way out without commenting on his work.

An old painter with a magnificent white mustache shook hands and said, "You have a feel for the human figure."

A fancy-stepping, non-objective painter, who drew about five hundred dollars a month so he would stay away from Cleveland, Ohio, and not embarrass his kin, said, "I'd like to see you loosen up a bit. However, the figure of the girl . . ." and he twirled the word like a top, "is freer than the others."

An old woman with a cane came by and said, "Young man, I love your landscape, the one of the creek and the fallen tree. I shall come back later and look at it."

To all these people Shaw said simply, "Thank you."

A young girl with short, blonde hair and a short, sexy figure said, "I just love your work. How long have you been painting?"

"All my life."

"Really? You mean you were just born with talent?"

"I can't rightly say about the talent, but whatever it is I guess I was born with it."

"We live in Denver. Have you ever been to Denver?"

"No."

"Well, we have some good artists up there. Do you know Salto Rabcook? He's just it. He's from New York. He's just the greatest!"

"I don't believe I do, but of course that doesn't mean anything."

"I don't quite understand."

"I mean, my not knowing him. I'm not acquainted with many artists. Just Dal over there." He pointed across the room where Dal was working and talking like hell to sell a painting to a gas company executive from Tulsa, Oklahoma.

"How quaint, you just knowing one artist. It's almost like Van Gogh. Are you like Van Gogh?"

Shaw blushed and twisted around and said, "Well, I ain't gonna cut off one ear on purpose."

"I like the way you talk. You talk like you're right from the earth."

"I just talk like that when I'm real drunk, real scared, or real sleepy."

"Oh, that's cute. I do hope I get to see you again before I leave."

Shaw said, "When are you leaving?" He was hoping it was now.

"Unfortunately, Monday. Will you be around tomorrow afternoon?"

"Sure," Shaw lied, "anytime."

She left.

The punch was gone, and there were still six or seven people left. Maybe the show could be called a middlin' success, aside from sales. It had been a total flop there. *Oh well*, Shaw thought. *It will hang for another two weeks. Lots can happen yet.*

It was dark all of a sudden. Shaw went into the bar to join Dal.

"I heard a lot of good comments, boy. We'll do some good yet. The word's out now. We have to start somewhere."

"Give me a drink," Shaw said to Gene, the bartender who was going to be a writer. He belted down the scotch. On top of all that punch, he could feel it coating the inside of his skull.

Soon Shaw went through the lobby on his way to the bathroom, and there was the old woman with the cane.

"Young man," she said, "how much is this? I can't read that small print." She stood in front of the landscape he'd painted in that glade, so highly secluded and so lovely and sad with memories.

"That's a hundred and fifty dollars," he said.

"I can't really afford it," she said, "but if you'll get me a blank check, I'll take it. It's a beautiful piece of work."

Shaw was as stunned as a man who'd just put a pistol to his head and pulled the trigger only to have the gun misfire. This old woman with the bent back, the lame leg, and the rheumy eyes instantly blossomed into a beauty that would have made Cleopatra envious enough to go to bed with a dozen poisonous snakes. She was a white rose with a heart bigger than a water buffalo's. She was the mother of the world and the patroness of all art that had ever been created. She'd held God's hand while he made the universe. Shaw loved her.

He folded the check, marked the picture sold, and kissed the old woman's hand five times. He still wouldn't know her name until he cashed the check.

The haze of alcohol and the thrill of his first sale sent him walking into the bar on sheep's wool and women's breasts. A great surge came into his throat, and he yelled.

Dal turned and clapped his hands and, smiling bigger than a clown, reached into his pocket and handed Shaw a check already made out. It said: FOR ANNA. A check for two hundred dollars from a great artist like Dal Holcomb. It was too much. Shaw grabbed Dal's forty-thousand-dollar-a-year hand and almost broke it.

Out the door he dashed. Out into the driveway and down into the desert, jumping and running through the night-blue sage. He yelled at the sky and waved a dozen kisses at the sapphire moon. He was a tiger bigger than a Percheron horse. He was an eagle who would fly past the moon so fast it would whirl in space like a blur. He was . . . He was . . . He was a selling artist. He, Shaw Spencer, had been paid cash money. Someone had liked his work enough to give real money for it. And he ran until he tripped and fell, then he got up and ran some more.

The cold air pushed the fumes from his head. He had the power of a diesel engine, the mind of Einstein and El Greco combined, and his spirit was all spirits that haunted the earth. It was his night. He howled again, and the coyotes heard—his brothers.

It was noon the next day when he woke up and looked in the mirror to comb his tousled, sandy hair. What had happened? In spite of the sales he felt like a grade-schooler sweeping an old folks' home. When would he be a real artist? Would it ever be?

Why wouldn't all this concern him so he could mature enough to at least look like he was an artist? When, if ever?

10

IT WAS THE DAY before the state elections. All around the village people were campaigning. Promises were made, favors were performed, and votes were bought with a drink, with a smile, with a lie, with a little leniency from the law officers, and in a thousand other ways.

It was a good time for those who bum drinks. Even better than the fiesta. For now the reddest-eyed, the weakest-kneed, the most ragged and filthy man on the street—or in the alley—had something to give in return. A vote.

Zacharias had even moved over to the small, front bar in the La Fonda Hotel de Taos. He was telling a group of his compadres who they must vote for.

"You know, my amigos, that the next county commissioner from our precinct will be none other than Rollo Martinez. This county has not known a better man than Rollo. He has character, this man. He has truth in his heart, even though he has been accused of many false things. There are those who say he sells supplies for all the county from his store while he is in office. I know this is not so, for I, Zacharias Chacon, son of Uvaldo Chacon," and he crossed himself, "witnessed with my own eyes," and he touched his thick glasses, "Rollo made a purchase in another store. And this purchase was done for a county truck. I was in Questa that day when the truck broke down, and as I said, 'with my own eyes,' and they are good ones, I heard this man call his own store, and when the parts could not be delivered through it for several days, he bought it right there in Questa. Now, you see, amigos, one must sort out the truth. I've even heard it said that Rollo hires all his own cousins on the road graders and such and makes them pay him twenty percent back in cash. Now, who could believe that of poor Rollo? Just because I, an experienced man with heavy equipment and a pardner of the rich gringo, Mr. Spencer, was turned down for a job, and he hired his brother-in-law instead, does not mean he's a crook. Far from it. No, amigos, it was just that Rollo and I had gone to the same school together many years ago, and he didn't want to show partiality to a friend. Everyone knows he hates his brother-in-law, and to drive a road grader is like being sentenced to hell for two years."

"Is that why he gave him the job?" asked Patrociño, the Woodcarver.

"That is right. It was a punishment."

Zacharias, with his gray hat, his glasses, and his light skin, stood out among his amigos like a white lion in a pen full of brown alley cats.

"But you have given me much confusion," said Patrociño.

"Ah, I must ask many pardons, Patrociño. Let me try to clear your mind for you."

"Clear mine, too, future father-in-law. It's clouded with misunderstanding as is Patrociño's," said the Lover.

Indian Tony, who had no intention of voting anyway, said, "Do not bodder, brudder. I savvy."

"No, Tony, let me tell you of an incident in our childhood that will make all of you realize that Rollo Martinez is a persecuted man. As you know, I spent my youth near Ranchos de Taos, carrying water from the creek. It was not much of a haul, only one-half mile downhill and one-half back up. Nothing for a man or boy to complain about. On washdays I made about ten trips. Now let it be said that what happened can only go to prove that Rollo must be reelected, for he is a man of skill and cunning. We need those in government. Do you think we want a bunch of dunderheads like ourselves?"

"No."

"No, Zacharias."

"Tell the story," said Patrociño, who ordinarily spoke very little.

"Yes, I'll tell the story. There was a little gringo boy, the son of an artist, who lived only a short distance from us. He was leaving soon for the East. A big city. I think Boston. We had played together many hours. I let him ride on the back of my goat, and he sometimes would gather eggs for me. Once in a while I'd let him carry a bucket of water for me, too. This boy, he liked mechanical things as I do. He said to me, 'When I leave, I'm giving you that big red wagon I got for Christmas. do you know what you can do with it, Zacharias? You can hook your goat to it and haul six buckets of water at one time.' Here I learned some of the value of properly placed words.

"So, you see, we worked as amigos. We worked our little hands to the blood, making a harness and fixing a lock on the handle of the wagon so it would not run away downhill. And we put axle grease on the wheels, and it was a dream to watch that goat. On washday I could haul enough water in one hour to last Mama the whole day. And when she wanted wood for the fire I could pull enough wood from the woodpile to the porch to do a whole month. And what fun to ride in this wagon. That goat was a stubborn animal. If I said 'whoa' or 'stop,' he'd pull the horns off his hard head. All this I learned in one week. My good friend Rollo learned this, too. And his grandfather had a goat better than mine. Do you know what that clever, smart Rollo did?"

"No, what?" asked the Lover.

Tony was adjusting his blanket, so he did not speak.

"He traded that artist's son a small sack of piñon nuts, a dead horned toad, and a promise to mail him a live mountain lion to Boston for that wagon."

"The feelthy rat," said Patrociño.

"The dog," said the Lover.

"Son of a goddamn bish," said Indian Tony in the white man's words.

"No, no, amigos. You must not say these words! Rollo did this all for my benefit. He knew carrying that water and that wood all day long would give me a good appetite and make me strong in the back. In fact, when I fell from the army truck in Germany, I would have been killed very dead if I hadn't had a strong back from carrying those great big, heavy, cold buckets of water until I nearly broke in half. I owe Rollo my life."

"I still have confusion," said Patrociño.

A man came among them then. He was short and fat with slicked-back hair, and he smoked a cigar.

"AYAAA, my friend, Lopez, where did you come from?" asked Zacharias in mock surprise.

"I've been here all the time you talked. You know my brother is running for office against Rollo Martinez?"

"AYAAA, that is right. I had forgotten," said Zacharias, taking off his glasses and wiping them on Indian Tony's blanket. It was doubtful if he could see anything at all afterward.

"Let me buy you a drink, Zacharias. You and your friends, too. You are an honest man. You've spoken the truth."

"Did I say one word against my friend Rollo?"

"Not one," said Lopez. "Just keep talking like that all day, tonight and tomorrow." He stuck out a fat hand to shake with Zacharias's large, flat one. Zacharias felt a folded bill in his palm, and he very casually dropped it into his pocket.

"I shall speak the truth forever, my friend Lopez. Here is to your brother."

"To all brudders," said Tony, raising his glass.

"I'm still confused," insisted Patrociño, shaking his head as he swallowed half a glass of wine.

The Lover saw a girl walk by the window and downed his wine in one large, drawn-out gasp then dashed for the door.

"Where do you go in such a hurry, son-in-law?"

"To pay the respects to your daughter and my wife in the very near future."

"A fine boy, that," said Zacharias with great contentment.

The Lover moved swiftly down the street after the girl. He twisted in and out of the crowd on the sidewalk as a snake goes through water.

"Alicia," he shouted.

She turned and smiled. "Hello, Flavio." There was an expectancy in her voice and an invitation. "I'm surprised to see you."

He moved very close to her. "I must talk to you about a very important thing."

"Shall we go to the Lucky Bar?" she asked.

"No."

"To my room?" she brightened.

"No, Alicia. No, it's even more important than that right now."

She knew that when he called her Alicia and spoke in that tone of voice he was in trouble. She turned her dark eyes to him and shoved her small breasts out.

"Where then?"

"Emilia's cafe."

"That bitch?"

"Yes. Be there in twenty minutes."

"What do you want, Flavio, to go to bed with both of us at the same time?"

"I'd like to try that, but today I don't have time. Just be there." He turned and hurried away. He'd already talked to Juanita, Emilia, and Maria, but he still had to contact Adele. She worked in the five and dime. It would be difficult to get her away if he were seen there. He would have to call. He'd saved a dime all day.

He dialed.

"Hello," came the voice. It was not Adele.

"This is Adele's brother. Her mother is sick. Is she busy?"

"Just a minute," the voice answered.

He smiled to himself. "Hello," he said as he heard Adele's voice. "Hello, Adele, this is your brother, Flavio."

He heard her breath being sucked in, and then she whispered into the phone, "What do you want, Flavio, you rascal."

"Listen, my sweet one, I told the lady your mother was sick and you must come quick. I said I was your brother."

"So?"

"Meet me at Emilia's."

"At that . . ." she said, catching herself, and then she hung up without further comment.

Well, he consoled himself, *even at election time women are more important.* The drinking would just have to wait until nightfall. *Oh, what a man gives up for women,* he thought as he eased his way to Emilia's Cafe.

Juanita was there in a booth with Maria. Emilia had served them coffee and now stood behind the counter, her arms folded and her jaw hard. All three glared at him like a judge does at a child murderer. He sat at the counter between the booth and Emilia.

"Some coffee, please, my pet."

Emilia snorted and said, "Aren't you afraid it will foul up your liver, Lover? It is a strange drink to you."

Juanita said, "He'll faint for sure. I can see it now. His stomach will explode at this strange liquid."

"You, my women, sound bitter. The coffee, please."

Alicia came in, stood a moment in the doorway, shrugged her shoulders, and sullenly joined the others in the booth.

"Coffee for Alicia, please."

"You are a generous man," Alicia snarled.

"In some ways I am," said the Lover, feeling the sweat break out all over him at the first taste of the hot coffee. It almost made him heave.

"Well," said Emilia, "what are we waiting for? It isn't money you want, is it? You've taken all I've had for three years. I can hardly keep this place open."

"Why, just look at all the business you have now," said Juanita, "and here comes another customer."

Adele entered hurriedly. She too stopped and surveyed the scene. Very little love or kindness showed in her eyes. She sat at the counter between the Lover and the door.

"I have to go soon," she explained.

"Coffee for Adele, please," said the Lover.

"Coffee for Adele. Coffee for Alicia. Coffee for Maria. Coffee for Juanita. Coffee for Emilia," Emilia sang as she did a little dance. "How many more can you supply with coffee, Flavio?"

Well, his time was upon him. If he didn't get the upper hand quickly, he was doomed. Things were getting out of control. He wished he had a speaking voice like his future father-in-law. It would help here. He could hardly have asked for his help, though, considering the problem.

The Lover stood up, balancing the hot cup of coffee and trying to show everyone how steady his hand was. He spilled about a third of it on the floor, and while they looked, he started his speech.

"Now, all you girls know that I love you. Each equally, but in different ways."

A loud *phhhttt!* burst across the room.

He remained undaunted and continued. "You cannot deny my words except out of meanness or jealousy. And you're all too fine for that. We've been through too much together to let a simple meeting interfere with what we have. Now, I could go on all day making excuses to you lovely girls . . ." He stopped just a moment and held his hat to his heart. "Ah, what a roomful of gorgeous women! Never on this earth has so much beauty and sweetness been under one roof."

All their mouths parted, and sounds to form words got only as far as the roofs of their mouths, for the Lover's voice was rising now along with his blood pressure and his determination to see the task through.

"It's been talked, rumored, and gossiped around this small village by loose tongues and jealous hearts that I've committed a terrible deed. It has been said," and he pushed his handsome head forward along with his loving hands, which were cupped as though he held a female breast in each of them, "it has been said that I've been trifling around you girls. It simply isn't so, even though it's come to my ears that some of you swear you have seen this with your own eyes. Now, what I want to know is if you're going to believe those lying eyes of yours or the man you love?" He gave each a steady look.

After this brief pause he continued, "It is some womanless man or some manless woman who has said this. I've been true to you girls. True! Blue! The fact of the matter is, I must get married."

He sped up his speech here, seeing only the calendar of the bull-fighter on the wall. "Through trickery and false accusations I've been forced to marry Rosita Chacon. She is with baby. It's not mine, but out of honor and friendship for my friend Zacharias I must sacrifice my freedom and make things right again. No, don't get upset, girls. We'll have even more time together. Zacharias has a very large check coming from the Veteran's Administration. When he gets it I'll buy you all presents, and we'll be together the long nights through."

Now he again looked each in the eye, trying to describe with a look, like an actor, the most precious of moments they had spent together. Whether it was the promise of gifts or the look he never knew, but with smiles so big all their mouths seemed one, they leaped at him and hugged him.

"My darling."

"My precious."

"My only one."

"My love."

And they spoke with a strange tone of both desire and fondness. Emilia gave everyone free coffee. He was sure they didn't mean a single word of it, but the day was saved. The Lover had come through again. He couldn't tell them now that he had intended to have them draw straws to see which one would be culled out for this year. He couldn't be that heartless now. Not just now.

11

APPROXIMATELY THREE BLOCKS NORTH, Shaw Spencer was putting the last stroke on Anna's behind—on canvas, of course. He had painted her recently in many poses: bending over a washtub scrubbing clothes, sweeping the floor, taking a bath, combing her hair in front of a mirror. All of them had been done in the nude. He tried her with clothes on, but, as he told Dal, "She just don't come off that way."

"Come rest, Anna. I know you're tired. Have some coffee," he said as he cleaned the paint off his hands. "Or is there something else you'd rather have?"

She said without hesitation, "Something else, Saw." She always called him this. The *h* somehow escaped her.

She pulled the old corduroy bathrobe around her round proportions while Shaw poured a drink of scotch over some ice. She took the drink, looked at him, and then she looked at the picture. Her eyes strayed from the picture back to him. This way she could tell if the painting was good or not. She could've stared at the canvas until it warped from age and wouldn't have known or cared if it was good.

"You like?" she asked, sipping the cold drink and pulling the robe away from her thighs just a little. She knew this sometimes made him passionate. She liked him best that way.

"Yes, I like." He smiled. He studied the finished painting and repeated, "I like very much."

He kept glancing at her brown thighs. She saw this, and the scotch turned warm in her stomach.

"Why do you like me?" she asked suddenly. "Is it because I make good pictures for you?"

"That's one reason."

"And is it because I make good love for you?"

"Not entirely."

"What then? Tell me."

"I don't know exactly. No one ever knows why they love. They just do. I know why I like you, though."

"Why? Please tell me, Saw."

"Well, you're a thief, and you don't deny it. You're a sometimes whore, and you admit it. I like the way you look on canvas and how you undress and how you feel. I like how you give more than you'll ever get in this world."

"You really like me then?"

"Didn't I just say?"

"But I don't understand all you say. Oh, the words, si, the meaning, no."

"That's what I mean. Any other female would have said she understood just to make me think she was deep . . . not that it's so deep."

"Deep?" and she glanced down at her stomach.

"No," he laughed. "Deep here," and he touched his head.

"Saw, why do you have so much money? Do you get it from your papa, or do you sell the pictures?"

"I don't have much money, Anna. I just spend like I do. I can never remember what it's for till it's too late."

"I love you, Saw."

"That's a fine thing to say, Anna," and he stared at her where the robe had fallen completely apart. He knew he must be kind to her, always, even if he didn't like her as much as he did now. She was his life projected there on the canvas.

Later, when she'd dressed, he gave her ten dollars and patted her on the plentiful butt that was both his art and his lust.

She headed for the Safeway store clasping the ten dollars like someone's life depended on it. Maybe hers did.

12

SHAW SPENCER HAD BEEN CURIOUS about the artist Hans Paap after watching his six-inches-at-a-time footstep. Well, it was actually more of a slide, a shuffle, than it was a step.

For him to get out of his studio to go after food or paint supplies must have been an enormous struggle. No one seemed to know his actual age. Some said he was around ninety. Others thought he was closer to a hundred.

For sure he was very old, and he was independent to a fault. Nevertheless, he was an enormously underrated painter in Shaw's mind. The studies in oil of Apache heads were powerful, rendered with a minimum of brush strokes, and the eyes projected life, a thinking life, right out of the frame, making the viewer feel that they were starting a conversation with the subject of the painting. This amazed Shaw all the more since Paap's heads were done in a minimum of painted area in the canvas. No one could experience their viewing and think they were photographic. How did he do it? Shaw was enthralled.

So he made his way up the little trail to Paap's studio with great anticipation. There was no way to get an automobile near the adobe structure. Only half a block from the Santa Fe highway and a block and a half from Taos Plaza, yet it felt wonderfully . . . isolated.

The studio itself took up eighty percent of the building.

The man who could barely make the short distance to the plaza opened the door to his home of art with animated enthusiasm.

"Ah, come in, young one. Come in."

"Thank you, Mr. Paap. I hope I'm not intruding on your work."

"No. No. I welcome your presence. Why do I have this honor?"

Shaw was surprised at his open humility and said, "Well, I saw a couple of your Apache portraits at the Taos Lodge. Mr. Holt showed them to me. I admired the seemingly simple way you created heads about to speak."

"Well, thank you, young man, that's good to hear. Especially from a young artist."

Shaw thought, *There it is again: "young artist."*

People all over the world in uncounted millions craved youth and longed for a younger appearance, but to Shaw his youth seemed a curse. He thought at times that there should be a law against judging works of art by the age or looks of the artist.

The Paap studio was large because the entire house was just a single room, except for a partitioned-off small kitchen and bathroom area.

Some observers might call the huge studio room a mess, but Shaw saw it as evidence of long hours of creativity. There were Paaps hanging along with works of other artists. He only recognized one Taos artist among them. There was Joseph Flock's portrait of an Indian posed with the Taos Pueblo in the background. Shaw observed that it had a little of the emanation of sound that Paap had somehow mastered.

Paap went right on painting, waving his brush at Shaw and motioning him to sit on an old couch that had a tattered red, white, and black Navajo blanket tossed across it.

Shaw wanted to look over Paap's shoulders so bad it hurt, but he respected the artist's private working space.

Paap stepped back and observed the Apache head on the easel. Then he made one last stroke, saying, "That's it. Better to know your last stroke is one too few instead of one too many."

Shaw heard the soft, muttered words and would never forget them.

After wiping his hands and dipping the brush in a jar of turpentine, Paap turned his bush-haired head and slitted blue eyes to Shaw and smiled, saying, "We must have a drink, huh, to celebrate your visit, huh."

He got a half bottle of gin and poured them each about two fingers in green drinking glasses. Shaw took it with much thanks even though he was not sure if the thick green glasses had ever been washed.

Then he stared at his portrait on the easel and said to Shaw, "What do you think, huh."

Shaw felt both embarrassed and privileged, but after a quick study he said, "I feel like I could have a good conversation with him if I could speak Apache."

This seemed to please Hans Paap, the artist from Germany and now Taos, New Mexico, for he swallowed the contents of the green glass after first clinking it against the glass held by Shaw, who followed suit.

"Another before it evaporates, huh."

Then raising the glass again in a toast, he said, "Mr. Spencer." He took a large sip and then continued. "There are only two things in this life that really matter in the finality," and he looked at an old photo in a stand on a cupola in the adobe wall, a striking woman, possibly thirty-five or forty years old, and said, "life and love, huh."

Shaw raised his empty glass and repeated, "To life and love, Mr. Paap."

Shaw stared out the great north window where Paap could turn his head from the painting on the easel and see the mighty Taos Mountains dominating all.

The rest of his visit became a warm blur, but it would stay with him for the rest of his life.

13

IT WAS THANKSGIVING DAY. The weather had sharpened, all the leaves had fallen, and the valley had now turned brown. It was the ugly time of year, before the snows came to give contrast. It was also the peaceful time of year, between the summer tourist season and the arrival of the skiers. Permanent residents were about the only ones here.

The travelers who arrived now were called visitors, not tourists, and they were usually made welcome. For one reason, the local populace needed business during the lull, and for another, everyone bows to money, even if the possessor is an idiot. The locals assumed that those who came now had considerable money. It wasn't likely they were just working people, and the weather was too cold to attract out-of-towners.

The Lover was unhappy this Thanksgiving. All his girlfriends were tied up with other members of their families. Zacharias had forced him to come to his house for the day. He had been invited to his Uncle Alfredo's, where there would have been a big turkey and much else—and besides, he had his eye on one of his cousins there—but he could not refuse Zacharias.

Zacharias was showing him Señor Buick for the twentieth time. "Have you seen my new car, son-in-law?"

"Yes."

"Ah, but look here. It has a sun visor, a gas cap, the tires are nearly all good, and listen to this," he declared as he crawled in and turned on the radio.

The rock and roll music blared forth so loud the eldest son, Romo, ran up and said, "Papa, I want to hear the football game on the radio."

"Who plays?"

"I can't remember, but the coach said it was to be a good one."

"Go ahead, my son," said Zacharias proudly, "but afterwhile we must run the car so the battery will not go bad."

"Okay, Papa."

"Flavio, would you like to go in and visit Rosita?"

"Afterwhile."

"When are you going to set the date for the wedding, my son-in-law?"

"Soon."

"You keep saying that. Next week we will have my check, then we will have a gigantic dance with much music and wine. Would you like a little drink, Flavio?"

"Might as well."

Zacharias went out behind the woodpile where there was an old hollow log. He'd hauled it long ago for firewood, but he'd discovered a better use for it. Reaching inside the log, he pulled out the Tokay.

"Here," he said.

"How do you manage to keep quarts and half-gallons now instead of pints?"

"My pardner, Mr. Shaw, wants me to feel good at all times. We're to open our construction company as soon as I get my check. He supplies me with the necessities."

"Why didn't he buy you a turkey for Thanksgiving then?" asked the Lover, glaring down his nose like a constipated prince.

"He is away to Santa Fe to take a picture to a gallery. Besides, you can't talk so loud," he said, glancing around toward the fence. "The Romeros next door think I'm rich. We must not let them know. It would only hurt their feelings. Would you like to play horseshoes?"

"Might as well."

So they pitched horseshoes. The Lover won with ease because he didn't care, so he was relaxed.

Mr. Romero was standing on his back porch watching his grand-children as they ran about, shouting and playing in the yard. Zacharias's children were there too.

Zacharias pitched a horseshoe and missed by a yard. Then, setting his eyes on the Romero house, he yelled in the direction of his house where Mama and Rosita were preparing the Thanksgiving meal. "Mama, that turkey done yet? Take a look at that turkey, Mama!" A little later he yelled again, even louder, "That turkey must be done by now, Mama. Don't get it too done."

Rosita came to the door and motioned to them.

Zacharias went over to the Romeros' fence and yelled at his kids so loud they stood straight up and quivered. They could have heard him in Talpa five miles away. "You children come and eat that turkey before that turkey gets cold."

The kids all rushed in the house. Zacharias followed the Lover, who walked very slowly.

Zacharias patted Mama on the biggest and best part of her anatomy, and then he walked over to the wood stove and looked in the big black pot.

"Mama," he said so the kids would be sure to hear, "you've cooked that turkey up in little pieces no bigger than a bean."

She looked at him, pushing the limp hair out of her eyes. "It's that wood you allowed me to cut. It gets too hot. Papa, the next time you buy us a turkey, get cooler wood to cook it with.

Rosita was holding Flavio's hand under the table. They all sat. Mama ladled out an extra-large helping of the "turkey" and tortillas to all and gave them each a smile full of love for dessert. Everyone knows that beans cooked with just the right amount of chile powder taste better than turkey. Most people had less that day.

14

THINGS HAD GONE WELL for Shaw his first year in Taos. He'd had a one-man show, sold some work, was involved in several affairs of the heart, and—what was more important to him—he had grown in his ability to paint what he felt. It wasn't realism he was after, nor was it abstraction of any kind. Lately what he'd been trying to incorporate onto his canvasses was the form of objects instilled with the mood of life, whether from the earth or the flesh. He was beginning to realize that these last two were the same. He was almost finished sketching the ceiling, too, but not quite.

Then events started happening to him that, at first, appeared disastrous. He had let a gallery owner in Santa Fe have nearly all his work.

The letter-thin man with the wavy hair, with the small mouth and swift tongue, had told him, "You'll be my only young, unestablished artist. The rest are old and settled and well-known. I'll build you into a nationally known painter in short order."

It had sounded really good, but then one day Shaw went to Santa Fe in the company of some St. Louis people who were interested in his work. They had arrived only to find the gallery closed, and it took Shaw all day to run down the truth. He found that although Mr. Allison was gone, his paintings were still in Santa Fe. Mr. Allison had sold them all, along with the work of several other artists, at little more than the worth of the frames, then vanished.

Shaw told the St. Louis group, "I'm out of business for now. Come back in about a year."

15

DURING THIS PERIOD of slight depression, Shaw sat in Skeezik's Drugstore one day reading the *Santa Fe New Mexican*. That particular issue was overloaded with murder stories and articles of violence.

Filled with desire and inspiration, Shaw rushed to his studio. He mixed up gobs of paint and gave a quick search around the room for a clean canvas. Finding none, he grabbed an already ruined landscape on the easel and started painting without even sketching. What emerged, completed in less than an hour, was one man beating the blood out of another. He sat and stared at the brutal work. Then he signed the back MAN by Shaw Spencer. He also signed the front.

When the picture was almost dry, Shaw took it to the Blue Door Gallery. This was the only gallery in town that would handle his work at this time. Canny Ross owned it.

"Look," Shaw said, "isn't that powerful? That's MAN!"

"Well, everyone has his own viewpoint," said Canny.

"Will you hang it?" asked Shaw. "It needs to be hung. People need to see it."

"Well . . . I don't know."

"Will you or not?" Shaw asked, leaning over the gallery owner with his nostrils sort of flaring in and out.

"Yeah, I guess so."

Shaw waited a week before he returned to the gallery. He wanted Canny to have plenty of time to get the public's reaction to his painting. He entered and saw that Canny was busy with a young, well-dressed couple, who were obviously potential buyers. Shaw wondered what they would have to say about his work.

He moseyed around, looking at other artists' work, not wanting to walk directly to his own. He circled the entire gallery and didn't see his painting. The thrill of a selling, young artist surged back and forth through him. He felt the joy come into his cheeks. Why, someone had bought it! He was the luckiest man in the whole of the universe.

He could hardly wait until the young couple left. He ran up to Canny.

"You've sold it! Who bought it?"

"Shaw, I didn't sell it."

"Well then, where is it?"

Canny pointed under a bench next to the wall. Shaw stared in disbelief. "What did you do that for? I never heard of a picture being hung under a bench. You expecting a bunch of midget art collectors in here? Couldn't nothing but a baby midget see that picture."

"To tell the truth, Shaw, some of the other artists complained about the picture. And truthfully . . . it seemed to nauseate the public so much I couldn't hang it."

"You couldn't hang it?" Shaw shouted. As soon as his blood started flowing again, he grabbed up his painting and rushed to the door. He stopped and shook it at Canny.

"You little cowardly son of a bitch!" he said.

And that is how Shaw Spencer lost both his galleries—one by thievery and one by cowardice.

He went on a two-day drinking binge. "To celebrate my freedom," he said. And he took his amigo Zacharias and eight or ten people with him. He had two fistfights, one which he lost, and he made love to three women besides Anna.

When he finally sobered up he went to the post office and found his mailbox full of envelopes with windows of pink.

He stared with sudden realization. He was broke, and not only that, he had one hundred and eighty dollars' worth of bad checks to cover.

Well, there wasn't any use sitting around and groaning about it. He'd had a lot of fun. The thing to do now was to get out and sell the three pictures he had left. By God, if he no longer had galleries to represent him, he'd treat his paintings just like Anna did her joy box. He'd peddle them just like apples, and he'd cover that ceiling canvas with glorious paint just like Michelangelo had done the Sistine Chapel. And the world would all come to gaze in awe at his creation. His alone.

Shaw Spencer, who looked more like a teenager than a mature, young artist, felt suddenly old and used up.

16

THE FIRST PERSON Shaw had to take care of was Holt of the Taos Lodge. He had sixty dollars' worth of Shaw's bad checks. On the way over there, Shaw remembered the story of Holt putting a hopeless alcoholic in jail for six months over a bad check for less than twenty dollars. The man had lived through the six months of the jail sentence, but he was so depressed on the day of his freedom he promptly drank himself to death.

Shaw didn't want any of that jail. Not the Taos jail, which was a combination of dungeon, sewer, and insane asylum.

Holt's attitude was cold. He took the checks out of the drawer and leaned across the front desk.

"I'm getting tired of this," he said, fondling the checks. "When can you take care of them?"

"Well," Shaw said, "I've got three good oils. Maybe we could do a trade."

"I don't know. Paintings are not worth much. Nobody'll buy them for more than the cost of the frame. Unless, of course, you've got a name."

"That last line is poetry," Shaw said, smiling.

Holt evidently didn't see the humor of it. He just jumped up and stuck the bad checks back in the drawer.

"I've got something to do," he said. "We'll see what we can work out later."

Shaw went into the bar and dug out enough money for a beer. He didn't like beer. His taste leaned more to brown whiskey. But . . . when broke . . .

He finished his beer. Fortunately a tourist, who was still drunk from the night before and still just as lonely, bought him another one.

Shaw thanked him and decided he'd get his paintings out of the pickup. It would be a miracle, but you never could tell when one of these drunk tourists would take a liking to a painting.

"That's pretty," the man named Bob said. "That's pretty. We don't have anything like that in Indiana. That's what I like, is those scenery pictures."

Shaw looked at the desert landscape in the soft light of the bar. It was pretty, but that was all. He didn't care right then. All he wanted was another beer and somebody to buy the picture.

"How'd you get started painting, anyway?" Bob asked, looking at him with red, watery eyes and rubbing his gray crew-cut head.

"I don't know," said Shaw. "I just couldn't help it."

"Where'd you go to school?"

"Chicago Art Institute."

"Is that so?"

"Yeah. It's a good school."

"I couldn't even paint a sign if I wanted to," Bob said. Shaw would have bet a quart of the best brown that Bob sure enough couldn't paint a sign, because that wasn't as easy as it sounds.

"Give us another beer, Josephine," Bob said to the short, blonde, lesbian bartender.

"The name's Jo," she said. "I hate Josephine." She also hated Bobs of all kinds.

"Okay, Jo, give us another beer."

She served the drinks, her blue eyes as cold as the frost on the beer bottles.

"No, sir," Bob said. "I couldn't draw a straight line."

"It ain't easy," Shaw said, swallowing beer.

Holt came in, pushing his massive frame across the quivering floor. He went behind the bar and started doing something. Holt was always doing something.

Shaw said, "Holt, here are the paintings." He set them, all three, up on the lounge tables.

Holt took a swift glance from behind the bar. Shaw stood and waited. Holt was still doing something.

Bob said to the blonde lesbian, "Jo, I wish I had some talent. It must be nice to be talented."

She didn't comment, trying to stay out of Holt's way. Then Holt walked from behind the bar, stopped for just a moment in front of the paintings, mumbled something, and moved on.

Shaw had no idea if he'd liked the pictures or what he said. He waited for six hours before he saw Holt again in the bar. He caught occasional glances of him moving through the lobby and in and out from behind the desk, but he didn't come around the paintings.

In the interim, Bob had forgotten the paintings and was telling Shaw about his wife.

"Now most folks don't realize that we've got nothing to do but work and make money. That's the way with my wife. You'd think she'd want something else besides money. Well, you'd be right. I got her a two-bedroom house. Since we've only got one kid, you'd think that'd be enough. Well, you'd be wrong. She wanted a three-bedroom and then a four-bedroom. And we've got two cars, and she belongs to seven clubs besides the PTA. And that ain't enough. I'm a deacon in the church. I belong to the Lions, the VFW, the Country Club, and I'm a troop leader in the Boy Scouts. Now how do you like that? It still ain't enough for that woman. I tell you she wants me to be on the board of directors of the Group for Bringing Opera to Indiana. Now how do you like that? Huh?"

"It just beats me all to hell," said Shaw, raising his tenth beer and trying not to hear Bob.

"Well, my daughter, she's getting ready to go to college. But a regular college ain't good enough for her or her mother. Oh hell, she's going to one of those private schools that costs enough to feed a barn full of hungry hay hands a whole year. She ain't going to learn any more there than in the university. Now, why do you suppose they insist on that?"

Shaw said, "It sounds better."

"It what?"

"Sounds better at the PTA."

"I don't get you."

"You never will," said Shaw.

"You trying to get smart with me or sumpthin'?"

"Forget it. Jo, give us a drink on me. Whiskey."

Jo phoned Holt at the desk. She knew Shaw had no money. Shaw was surprised when she served the drinks without question. But then he had lots to learn, and he caught on to quite a few of the world's tricks before the night was over.

It was midnight when Holt finally took time to talk trade with Shaw. He had the bad checks with the pink slips sticking out of his shirt pocket like a streetlight. Shaw was blurry-eyed drunk. He'd charged twelve dollars' worth of drinks while going through the long wait. The markup was high on brown whiskey. Holt was that much ahead just to start the trade with.

After moaning awhile about how bad business was and how many bad checks he got a month and how high taxes were and how sick his big, fat, complaining wife had been, Holt finally gave Shaw six dollars in cash, returned the sixty dollars in checks to him, and called the bar well paid. In return he received two paintings, which he sold before the year was out for five hundred dollars cash. He hid the money from that sale from both his wife and the Internal Revue Service. Mr. Holt was admired as a businessman.

Shaw took the deal, bought Bob a drink, and went out to look for Anna.

17

SHAW WALKED BOLDLY into the art supply shop, although in all honesty his heart was doing the tango in his breast and his stomach was jumping.

He spoke to the laughing lady.

The laughing lady spoke back, "Ohhhhh, hoooo, oh, ho, ha, I hear you've been selling lots of work."

"That's true," said Shaw with some dignity and pride. He'd sold six portraits and nudes of Anna for a total of ninety-seven dollars in cash, six free meals, twenty or thirty drunks, a fifteen-year-old sewing machine, and a rifle. He traded the latter two to Holt for sixteen dollars' worth of drinks and a cheap Indian bolo tie he gave to Indian Tony for posing. But he could say only four words that fit his artistic endeavors. *He was surely selling.*

Shaw promptly ordered some canvas, some new brushes, and paints of all kinds . . . Everything he would need for a spell.

Laughing lady just bubbled over with joy and giggles while she wrapped the supplies. A sale of this size was rare, even in a town full of "artists."

"Will that be, ha, ha, heee he, all?"

"Yes'm," he said, picking everything up in his arms and heading for the door. "Charge it!"

"But . . . but . . . but . . ." she said, and for the first time that year she forgot to giggle.

Shaw walked straight out to his pickup and felt a cold chill run around on his back like a man must feel when he walks across a clearing in front of enemy machine guns. He didn't look back though. He got in the old pickup and almost ripped the gears out leaving.

He had to find Anna and get some paintings done. It seemed those he did of her were much better than his landscapes and townscapes, and they were much better than the occasional portraits he did of Indian Tony. To his eager satisfaction they sold better, too.

Since his phone had been removed and his electric lights had been cut off, he had less to worry about. The coal-oil lantern was not strong enough to paint by, so he had to get to work as early as possible during the day. About all he had to worry about now was his rent, the small loans company taking his pickup, and getting enough extra paint for the ceiling, where he must eventually paint everything in the world. He'd finally made one payment on the pickup, but if he didn't have the other by tomorrow, the man had told him, "We'll be forced against our wishes to impound the truck, and unfortunately, young man, this will involve attorney's fees, extra interest, and penalties."

The last few months Shaw had decided it was extra interest and penalties that killed most people, instead of disease, accidents, and outright murder.

He found Anna in the Lucky Bar, and though she was weaving, dancing, and shaking her hindquarters at random in the middle of the floor, he convinced her to leave.

She crawled into the pickup after several faltering attempts.

"Didn't you see old cigar-smoking Varos from the hardware store?"

"Yeah."

"Well, why you no leave me alone?"

"I told you, Anna, I need you now. I've got to get out a canvas today."

"But ol' Varos was all ready to go to the Sagebrush. He pays good— sometimes three dollars. On the fourth of July he gave me five."

"I realize that's a lot of money, honey, but you'll just have to trust me to do better by you. I swear that by morning I'll have ten dollars for you."

She leaned, or rather fell, over against him as he turned the corner to the studio.

"I do not care. I only tease with you. I will pose for twenty-seven days and nights."

"Thanks, honey," he said, reaching around her shoulders and squeezing her.

They alighted swiftly. Shaw stepped out. Anna fell out. He helped her to her feet and led her toward the door while he gathered up the art materials. He glanced up longingly at his canvas ceiling, then he shrugged, placed the canvas on the easel, and picked up a piece of charcoal. He looked hard at the vast, blank space, at the emptiness, the nothingness that challenged him. He had to take this white nonentity and put flesh and breath and bone and blood, light and darkness into it. He had to instill it with life.

Anna knew what to do. She pulled her dress over her head. Her mighty, plump breasts shook free and pulled at her shoulders. She twisted from her silk panties, frayed around the edges by time and eager hands. She turned and looked at him, waiting for him to pose her.

He walked over with a broom and a dustpan. "This is going to be difficult, Anna," he said. "Now look, I want you to pose like this. Okay?" And he bent over, sweeping into the dust pan with one hand, her hind end toward the canvas at about a three-quarter angle.

Anna tried it, and she had some difficulty adjusting her feet so she wouldn't wobble about.

Finally she had to plant them firmly apart.

Shaw thought it was awkward but had a primitive, posed quality about it. He painted. Anna would hold the position until her alcoholic blood filled her head, and then she'd fall.

Shaw never quit painting, however, because as soon as the whirling slowed in her brain, Anna would scramble back into position. He painted swiftly, accurately, and with such feeling for Anna's struggle. He had to, that was all.

At last Anna fell and stayed down, rolling over on her back with her legs spread apart like the whore she was. She slept.

Shaw finished the canvas and washed the paint from his hands. Then he looked at the canvas with a fresh eye. It was good. He took it down and, without so much as a glance at Anna, walked out to the pickup. He talked to it as a cowboy does his horse.

"Well, ol' red, how do you like this picture? If we're to remain pardners, someone besides myself has gotta like it, and quick.

He drove carefully so the canvas wouldn't fall and smear. He parked the pickup and walked into the Taos Lodge. Holt grunted to him from behind the desk.

"Painting?"

"Just finished one."

Holt perked up and became slightly more friendly at this. He was already mulling over several things in his mind. If Shaw had brought the wet, unframed picture with him, that meant he was broke. More than that, it meant he was in trouble. He could probably steal it for a pittance before morning. Of course, once in a while Shaw would sell a picture to a traveler.

This way the twenty-five percent commission would be less than Holt could make on a resale, but Shaw would be forced to buy more drinks. Either way he couldn't do anything but win. It pays to be a businessman.

Shaw went out to the pickup and got the wet, unfinished picture. Holt looked at it and closed his eyes so Shaw couldn't see the greed. Holt knew nothing of art and never would. But he knew the taste, the feel, and the smell of money like he did his wife's breast. This picture represented money. Money.

Shaw no longer kidded himself about a quick, honest trade with Holt. He went straight to the bar and perched himself on the stool like a hungry eagle on a bluff looking for a victim on the prairie below.

Jo looked at the picture admiringly. She had seen dozens of canvases of Anna that Shaw peddled, but she'd never seen Anna. Shaw saw to that. He didn't want his model to become corrupted or anything like that.

Jo said, "I like it."

Shaw started to respond, but he caught himself. He mustn't infringe on Jo's operations any more than she did his. People needed one another in this world no matter how varied their inclinations.

He ordered several drinks. Jo put them on the tab. He played the jukebox with his last quarter and stole half a package of cigarettes from Jo.

He waited and waited, but no one but an Indian, and a tourist who only wanted a coke, came into the bar. He sat and brooded because he'd had a good start on his ceiling a few months back, but now it was neglected like a garden full of weeds. He spent most all his time waiting for a dollar to float by.

He'd arrived just after lunchtime, and it was now three-thirty. It wasn't long until morning, and then he'd be afoot.

"Well," he said, "that's the life of an artist."

"Huh?" Jo said blankly.

"I said, the life of an artist is wild and free, and full of sport and fun."

"Are you kidding?" she said.

"Yeah, honey, I'm kidding ol' Shaw, not you."

And then he heard it. It was a noise. It came by the desk and into the bar. It was female.

Shaw's eagle's claws grasped the barstool until his knuckles turned ice cold, his nostrils flared, and his eyes turned bright, ready for an instant kill. In his case that meant ten hours.

They saw the picture before he turned, and they said, "I like that," in the same soft southern drawl. "I really like that."

"It reminds me of dear mother," one laughed.

One of them reached out to touch it, and Jo screamed, "No, it's wet!"

Shaw sat very still. He'd seen the hand going for the background and not the figure. This was to his advantage. It put them under obligation and in no way hurt the painting.

"Oh, I'm sorry," said the forty-five-year-old brunette with the yellow-brown eyes of a barn owl. She held her hand up with the oil paint smeared across two fingers. She walked toward the bar, and Jo handed her a napkin.

"I'm so sorry," she said again. "Whose is it?"

Jo pointed to Shaw.

She looked at him and said, "I guess you'll make me buy it."

He said, "No, ma'am, not unless you want it." He knew he had a deal. But the ritual had just started. The bands were just now playing. The preliminaries were commencing.

"Would you care to have a drink with us? Are you sure the painting isn't damaged?"

He sat down at a table with them and said, "Nothing that I can't fix."

The woman ordered drinks. Shaw looked at the blonde, who was perhaps five years younger than her companion.

"I'm Erline," she said, "and this is Millie."

"Hi, I'm Shaw."

Shaw ordered a scotch and water. He watched Millie take the billfold from her purse and remove the hundred-dollar bill. There was a very neat stack of new bills about a quarter-inch thick in the billfold. *If these are all hundreds,* he thought, *this woman is purely loaded.*

Millie settled down to drink her salty dog and Erline did likewise. Shaw noted with detailed observation that her fingers were covered with huge diamonds and that they both used too much makeup to cover their rather attractive facial wrinkles. Millie was fairly well established, as far as breastworks were concerned, but her hindquarters couldn't compare to Erline's, who wore tight black slacks.

Neither one was too bad—they both had pleasant natures. So he could just play it by ear and take the first one that fell. Hell, he had to sell the picture. That was all. Why torture himself with the means. Instead he decided to enjoy it the best he could. Holt made him pay enough each time he sold a painting—in time and tension—for the worth of ten love affairs.

"Are you married?" Millie asked, shifting the sunglasses on her nose.

"No."

"Why, I expected a talented and good-looking young man like you to be taken."

"Talent's not enough in this world, honey," he said, smiling so as to keep them from thinking he was wising off.

"What does it take?"

"Well, a feller has got to be a businessman."

"To get married? Why, I'm sure lots of painters are married who aren't businessmen."

"Not for long, honey."

"You mean they just can't get along with their wives?" asked Erline.

"That's no trouble; they just can't get along with the world."

Before they could ask him "why," he slipped a quarter from Millie's change and went to the jukebox. Millie left the table in search of the powder room. On the way back she stopped where he was still studying the jukebox selections. That was just the way he'd planned it. The decision-making was over.

"Come on," he said, and he waltzed her off and around the barroom. He held her close and felt how soft she was, and he could feel her making little short snorts of her breathing already. Hell, this was a cinch. He was in.

They went back to the table, and he knew he had her by the way she was beaming.

When she caught her breath, she ordered three drinks and asked, "How did you happen to become a painter?"

Well, there it came, he thought. He was used to it now. Might as well play along and get it over with.

"I don't know . . . I just couldn't help myself. I needed to paint just like one needs to go to the bathroom. It was unavoidable." This got to them. They understood this in some vague way.

Then the next question came, right in order.

"Where did you go to school?"

He told them, then he added, "Of course, I've learned a lot more from just painting than I ever did from studying."

He was beginning to get the answers now.

"I couldn't draw a straight line," Millie said, looking at Erline.

"Me either," said Erline.

"Hardly anyone can," said Shaw. "A straight line is very difficult to draw."

Nine times out of ten he found this ended that particular subject. It worked this time.

There was more dancing and a lot more drinking, then finally Millie leaned against him and said, "Erline's gone to take a nap. She'll be out cold. I know her."

Here it comes, thought Shaw. *By God, this is fine. I'm not even going to have to ask her.*

"Look, darling," Millie said, placing the palms of both her hands on his chest and looking up into his eyes. "I'm going to the room. Now, why don't you wait about fifteen minutes and come up?"

He kissed her good and steady like she wanted, and then he said, "I'll be there. I couldn't stay away."

She turned, tossing her head back as she did when she was eighteen, and said, "Oh yes, darling, and bring the painting. I've decided I want it."

Shaw smiled sweetly at her, then he sat back on his perch to finish his fifteen-minute wait. He took the painting and went to Millie's room. Jo watched him go, half jealous and half mad. She'd seen this happen before.

The room was almost dark. He could hear snoring coming from one of the two beds.

"Millie?"

No answer.

His eyes adjusted to the light. Erline was passed out with her clothes on. She was the one snoring. Millie was stretched out on the next bed, naked except for her sunglasses. As his eyes fully adjusted to the light he saw that she had thrown her clothes and bag on the floor like the scattered dung of a running cow. Tossed about on the floor was money. Money. He bent and picked up the bills. He stuck exactly half of these in his pocket and put the rest back in her purse.

He sat on the bed beside her, reached out to take the sunglasses from her sleeping face, and then pulled his hand away, leaving the glasses still in place. Hell, he didn't want to make love to her stark naked when she had no knowledge of it. He felt, though, that he must love her. It was part of the unspoken bargain. He'd tell her how good it was the next day even though she'd never know the difference.

Afterward he tiptoed to the door and went out, leaving the painting behind.

He felt exceptionally well. It was the first time he'd sold a picture for nine hundred dollars cash. He bought a bottle at the bar, gave Joe a ten-dollar tip, and at her caustic, "Fast worker, huh?" he answered, "When necessity demands, honey." He drove home, walked in, and lit the kerosene lamp.

Anna was still on the floor where he had left her. It struck him as funny that he'd left Millie in exactly the same position on the bed.

He got Anna by the arms, dragged her over to the bed, and propped her up against a pillow. She opened her eyes.

"Saw," she said, "did you finish peecture?"

"Yeah, honey. I finished. Tomorrow we'll do another one."

He walked across the room to mix them a drink, leaving her to stare with total amazement and unbelief at the hundred-dollar bill in her hand. They'd both earned it.

18

ZACHARIAS WAS NOT VERY DRUNK. This was, of course, unusual. He opened the door and stood a moment, looking at Mama. She was ironing for Guzman the artist. The sweat had caused her dark hair to stick to the sides of her face as if it were glued there. Zacharias thought how beautiful she was. There was something about her sweating over the ironing board every day that made a big love feeling in his heart. And, of course, that fanny as wide as a door was a marvel to the beholder. He slapped her fanny with a long swing. Mama just pushed some of the sweat off her forehead and said, "Here, here," but a tiny little fleeting smile danced across her lips and around in her eyes. She wondered why Zacharias was home at this time of the day. He seldom was.

He said, "Mama?"

"Yes."

"You got any money, Mama?"

"No, not till Guzman comes after the ironing. I'm on the last shirt now," she'd added for encouragement.

"I've got to go have a paper notarized for the government," he told her. "It's very important. It concerns the check," he lied.

Mama understood that it was a lie whose only purpose was to make it sound better. She knew that he did not lie to hurt her.

"Then why don't you take these clothes to Guzman?"

"Walk? You know the car is being fixed."

"Si, he lives only three blocks away on the Loma. You walk that every day to the plaza. Sometimes twice."

"AYAAA, Mama, you are right. I forget sometimes. My mind is so busy with plans for Mr. Shaw and our construction company."

"Si," she said, and she handed him the entire ironing load, hung on wire hangers. "It will be three dollars," she said.

"Ah, Mama," he said, and he tried to kiss her on the neck. Mama laughed and backed away, saying, "Don't mess up the ironing, or you might never get the papers notarized."

"Right again, Mama. If the world would just listen to you, Mama, there'd be no more wars. Everybody would have happiness all over."

"Get out," she said, embarrassed at this compliment.

"Si, I must go now. Ah, Mama, mine—later today I'm going to bring you a present. I'm going to all the artists to ask for loans until Mr. Shaw and I get our business going. It will only take a few days once the check comes."

Mama was busy now, doing the ironing for her own family.

He eased through the door, being careful with the fresh ironing, realizing it was a tiny pot of gold he carried in all its cleanliness.

He called back through the screen, "Remember, Mama, a present."

She said nothing, knowing he wouldn't bring her a present, but warmth came between her breasts because he thought of it at all. Thoughts were everything, she felt; anyone could do deeds. What you thought was what you were, and her man of the alcoholic blood was full of fine thoughts. This she believed.

Zacharias walked with purposeful strides past the school and down the Loma to the gate of Guzman the artist. A big dog barked and acted as if he would remove a foot from Zacharias. Zacharias stood his ground firmly behind the gate and said to the dog, "If you could see this enormous shoe of mine, dog, you'd run and hide in the flowers. The shoe I wear is big enough to make a garage for the Jeep. Dog, if I, Zacharias, should kick you, it could be three days before you get back to Taos. You'd go so high, the clouds of the Sangre de Cristo Mountains would look like a puff from a stinking corncob pipe."

Guzman came out and yelled at the dog. "Here, what's the matter with you, Herman? Come on in. He won't bite."

And sure enough, when Zacharias entered the patio, the dog wagged his tail and wanted to jump up on the ironing. Zacharias leaped back and then, to make it safe, he swiftly handed the clean clothes to

Guzman. Now they were the artist's responsibility. Zacharias knew that artists were fools—with the exception of Shaw, of course, who was his business pardner. They all liked to think they were kindhearted and broad-minded. If there was anything an artist liked, it was to show kindness to a downtrodden Indian or Mexican. Especially the artists from the East. That was fine with Zacharias. Today he had decided to make life better for the artists. He would just call on all he could find and give them the opportunity to help a poor, downtrodden Mexican, who also happened to be part German.

Guzman was a walking owl behind his thick glasses. A short, paunchy, arrogant owl, but he invited Zacharias into the huge, beamed living room, so full of paintings, with a false humility that delighted Zacharias's thirsty heart.

Mrs. Guzman met him with a grin like an adobe wall in a state of disrepair. She had the shoulders of a wire coat hanger, hips like a small, cheap picture frame, and legs that seemed about to fly into splinters. Zacharias knew that she was very rich and that Guzman would be right back to peddling things—whatever it was he used to peddle— if it wasn't for her. But he didn't care, and oddly enough he liked her.

"Ah, the ironing. Zacharias, come in, come in." Zacharias was already in, but he stepped further in. "Here, sit down, dear fellow. Let me get you something. What would you like, dear fellow?"

Zacharias thought for a minute, then he screwed up his face and took off his sweaty, old gray hat. All the time he knew it made no difference as long as it was wet and alcoholic.

"Scotch and water?" she asked, helping.

Zacharias snapped his fingers at the revelation. "Si, si!"

"Boris," she said, "that'll be two scotch and waters, and a light gin with tonic for me."

Zacharias looked around at all the paintings. If you looked awhile you could tell that the blue parts were mountains and the red and yellow parts were either sky or desert. He reasoned that where the blue parts came to a point must be the sky, because that's how mountains looked up in the sky.

Boris left to mix the drinks. Mrs. Guzman, with a grin that pushed her eyes into tiny wrinkled slits that made her fifty-five-year-old face look a hundred and five, said, "How's your family, Zacharias? Is the wife in fine fettle?"

Zacharias didn't know what fine fettle meant, but he said, "Si, Mrs. Guzman, she's got a lot of fine fettle. That Mama is some Mama."

The grin lessened slightly as Boris entered with the glasses.

"Sit down, my boy," said Boris. "Sit down and enjoy your drink."

Zacharias wondered why these people were always saying, "Enjoy your drink," "Enjoy your meal," and "Enjoy yourself." Wasn't that what everyone did with a drink in his hand? There was a lot of difference in holding a cold scotch or holding a hot shovel handle. How could a man so blessed, trying with all his might, keep from laughing out loud.

They talked on about a lot of little nothings, which Zacharias answered carefully and kindly.

Mrs. Guzman, as Boris called her, looked out a huge picture window and sighed. "Ah, the Taos Mountains," she said. "D. H. Lawrence was right. There's none in the world like them. There's no place like Taos, right, dear fellow? We're going to Barcelona for a year, but we'll miss Taos. Yes, we'll miss Taos."

Zacharias wondered why in the hell they were leaving for a year then. He didn't know that they had to just because it sounded good. They could say, "Oh, because it was charming, but we're glad to be back in Taos."

Soon Boris got them all another drink. They had stopped insisting on Zacharias's enjoying himself.

Suddenly Mrs. Guzman got up and walked her wooden body into another room, excusing herself to make a call, and then she came back and apologized five times for the fact that they'd forgotten a luncheon engagement in town and must, regretfully, get ready.

"How much was the ironing, dear fellow?"

Zacharias said, "I've forgotten."

"Ah well," she said, handing him five dollars. "Will this do?"

Zacharias took the five dollars, thanked the grinning pair for the drinks, and got the hell out of there.

Things had started off like he had a long-term lease on heaven:

two large belts of scotch in his thirsty belly and a fiver to grease his hungry pocket. He was tempted to head for the plaza right now, but suddenly he felt he knew what the artists were always talking about when they used the word *inspiration*. It was the same when you were hot with the dice. He was hot! Why, he'd even go and try out the wild man, the artist Zeckdorf. It was only a few blocks downhill, past the school again, up behind Funk's five and dime, past the bank, then down a narrow alley of adobe houses, some covered with concrete and all dirty, to Zeckdorf's studio and home.

He knocked on the door. Zeckdorf yelled, "Who is it? Come in."

Zacharias entered.

Zeckdorf was painting. He didn't look up. He was dribbling paint on a canvas stretched out on the floor. Zacharias marveled that he could drip the paint in such idiotic circles and still keep it on the canvas and off the floor. That took real skill. The man was a genius. Zeck, as he was called by both his enemies and his friends, emptied the can with a flourish and looked up, his smiling eyes gleaming about a mustache as big as a hair brush. Zacharias was tall, but Zeck looked down on him. His sickly blue eyes kept opening so wide Zacharias half expected the lids to split, and then he'd squint them almost shut and twitch one cheek. His brown, dry hair stood up in little patches around the top of his head like that of a discarded doll.

His smile vanished. "It's you," he said. "You never did come after my laundry, man."

Zacharias had forgotten that he'd promised a few months before to take care of Zeck's laundry for two weeks in exchange for two dollars. He'd honestly forgotten after deciding that Zeck had no interest in cleanliness anyway.

"My brother, he die," Zacharias said, trying to sound humble and ignorant.

"Oh," Zeck said, grabbing up a full can of yellow paint. Now he was circling the canvas, tiptoeing like a ballet dancer about to jump on something helpless. Zacharias watched him a moment, thinking maybe he might be dangerous. Then Zeck started piling the paint in little blobs. He ran a thin line or two between the blobs.

"How is Taos?" he asked Zacharias bluntly.

It was hard for Zacharias to give an answer to a man who lived in the very center of it.

He said, "Oh, about the same as ever. The *touristas* will start soon now."

"Tourists. God uh mighty, man, is that all you people in Taos think about? You curse the Texans when they're here and curse them when they don't come."

Zacharias wondered why the artist said *you people*. He could remember Zeck having been here at least ten years. He thought he'd try a new approach to please Zeck.

"Oh, the touristas don't come to see the mountains or the streams, or the beautiful desert; they come to see you artists."

Zeck blew about a teaspoonful of something out of his nose with a snort like four braying jackasses. "Artists? What artists?" he screamed. "Let me tell you, man." He dashed the can of yellow until it was empty, leaped up, dived across the room, and snatched a can of brilliant red from a shelf. "Let me tell you something, man. Taos isn't full of artists. It's loaded with businessmen who paint, and remittance men who are paid to stay away from home. All the artists are dead or gone except me, and this cruel place will soon do me in." His voice rose even more. "They hate me—they hate all Spanish Americans—and they crap and step on the indigenous people like pissants. Hell, prejudice. I guess so, man. It's reversed. The kindest heart."

Zacharias started to open his mouth and defend his hometown, but even if he hadn't suddenly realized that his purpose here was to acquire additional funds for Mama's present, he would have still been drowned out, for Zeck roared on.

"This place is a conglomerate of amateur painters, total fakes, little groups that run around taking turns giving one anther prizes, and old women in pants who don't know vermillion from burnt umber."

"My pardner, Mr. Shaw, is pretty good, no?"

"You spread his name around like plaster, man. It's too early to tell, but he has signs. Only the slightest indication so far. Listen, man," he said, standing now with the red dripping all around like scattered blood in a slaughterhouse. "No one would even know Taos existed if Kit Carson and D. H. Lawrence hadn't stopped here awhile. It'd be just another little cheap tourist trap."

Zacharias had just decided not to listen. He looked off into another room and could see a woman sitting in there reading a tiny book. Her hair hung down very far, and it suddenly occurred to Zacharias that it was covering the most important parts of her nude body. Her skin was pale and looked like milk about to clabber. She didn't move. Not even her eyes seemed to move as she stared at the book. It must be a very interesting picture in that book, thought Zacharias. He heard Zeck's voice raving on, but he refused to discern the words. He studied a big iron sculpture of what he supposed was a man. Its neck was eighteen inches long, one leg ran out like bent barbwire, and it had a badly broken back and a little head the size of a shriveled apple. Suddenly Zacharias felt very sorry for Zeck. He believed Zeck said and did things as he truly saw them. A man who saw other men like that was to be pitied from the depths. He had a sudden desire today to do something to soften the harsh, distorted life that must surely range before this man's eyes, but he didn't have a chance.

Zeck clapped his hands loudly. The long stretch of hair and bones rose from the chair and entered the studio.

She walked sleepily, shoulders sagging around her little breasts, over to Zeck. Zeck was not even looking at her. But Zacharias was. The woman was surely as tall as he was. Suddenly Zeck's head shot up and became rigid. A sort of growl came from his throat. He leaped completely over the canvas and threw the woman hard against the floor. She didn't seem to feel any pain, but she lay stretched out as if she were unconscious. Zacharias was sure the fall had sent her into that state. Still growling, Zeck rolled her over and grabbed the back of her hair in one hand, then he put his right arm under her legs, whirled about twice, and threw her sliding across the canvas, breasts first. He ran back, took the same hold on the paint-smeared girl, and danced her around the canvas, touching her small breasts to it here and there. Then he discarded her on the floor. Zacharias wanted to help her up, but considering all things, he decided against it. It didn't matter; she got up anyway and started wiping herself off with the same dirty rags and turpentine. Now Zeck stood breathing hard, his eyes opening and closing so hard it was difficult to tell what was what.

Zaharias could tell that Zeck was pleased with the mess on the floor, and knowing artists all these years he knew he must make his move, now. He had to talk and act very ignorant here. That was the secret with this kind of artist. "I . . . I sorry. My brother, he die. And the laundry not done, amigo. But this I promise you now, to do four weeks laundry for only two dollars. I pick it up mañana when my car will be fixed."

The artist reached over on a shelf and said, "Here. Four weeks, now that's a deal, man." His wide, putty-blue eyes were still blinking at the canvas. "No more dead brothers, you promise me, man."

Zacharias took the paint-stained bills, headed for the door, and shouted back, "I promise my brother no dies again."

Then, as he danced down the road, he muttered to himself, "He won't die again until next year."

19

ZACHARIAS WALKED INTO LOWELL'S STORE, which sat at an angle across the street from the Taos Inn. He had seven dollars in his possession and an enormous thirst. He knew that he had to get the present for Mama now or it would never happen.

His throat was so dry he could hardly talk. A man and his wife, both about fifty, with the shrunken souls of do-gooders from the Bible belt, ran the place. Zacharias was not the usual customer. The smell of alcohol shriveled their little souls further, but he didn't notice anything but a man and woman who could help him in a moment of deepest need. There was nothing on earth as deserving as his wife, Mama.

The woman was about to grab her sagging but quantitative breasts and yell, "Out!" when she saw the money in Zacharias's hand. At that instant her expression changed. In fact, her whole bearing changed, and she sold Zacharias a rebozo—which she had imported from Mexico at ninety-two cents—for five and a half dollars. Her husband stood by beaming kindly, like a church deacon thinking of his mistress while passing the collection plate.

"Wrap it good," Zacharias said. "It is for Mama."

The lady put the money in the cash register first, and then she wrapped the yellow and red rebozo up in brown paper.

"There," she said, handing it to him and turning her head so as not to breathe any of the fumes that emanated from Zacharias's body.

Zacharias thanked her then, about four times, as he backed to the door and out. The two merchants looked at each other and breathed almost normally again.

Zacharias was still dry, but he had a momentary lift as he walked toward the Lucky Bar. He still had a dollar and a half. He had two quick glasses of wine and showed the package to the bartender and smiled a little importantly. "A gift for Mama," he said.

The bartender said, "A new mop head?"

"No, the finest rebozo from Spain. Another glass of wine you unseeing fool."

The bartender served a little more graciously this time, realizing his joke had somehow offended Zacharias. He didn't want to do that. Zacharias created, all told, more business for him than anyone in Taos.

The bartender lied. "A Patrociño Barela, the Woodcarver, was looking for you."

"For me?"

"Si."

"I must, of course, wonder what for?"

"He did not say, but he seemed very anxious." The bartender could tell that this did indeed make Zacharias feel better—that someone wanted to see him. Anyone. Truth was, the bartender hadn't seen Patrociño in three days, when he'd bought two bottles of Tokay wine and left.

"In that case," Zacharias said, "I think I'll go back to the Ranchitos and see if I can find him."

He walked confidently, exuberantly, to the northeast corner of the plaza and turned down Kit Carson Road. He walked fast, with long strides, and turned at the Ranchitos Bar toward Patrociño's woodshed. Dogs barked at his strange pace. No one walked that fast and purposely in Taos.

He heard dogs barking again, and he told them all, "It is said that the Indians love fresh dog meat, and they are going to have a glorious feast this night if you keep that sound of the devil yapping from your crazy throats." The dogs barked on.

He knocked at the door of Patrociño. His wife, one of those people Zacharias disliked, came to the door. This was a woman of no great beauty, being built somewhat like a bent refrigerator. Her head was round on the sides like a pair of half-moons and flat on the top like a row of rulers. Two teeth showed under an upper lip that snarled to the side like she had just spit out a bitter, poisoned plum. Her eyes were so small Zacharias always felt like taking a screwdriver and prying them open.

"What you want?" she grunted.

"Uh, Patrociño has a message for me."

"He's out there for two, three days now. I no see him. Maybe he drunk or whittling silly things like always."

Zacharias was struck with a sudden and strange wonder for a man like Patrociño, who gave so much beauty to the world and received so much ugliness in return, as exemplified by this creature he called his wife. Zacharias marveled that Patrociño spoke of her in the kindest manner always.

"I'll go see," Zacharias said politely, touching the brim of his old gray hat.

"Give him a message from me," she said. Zacharias hesitated, waiting. "Tell him to go to hell."

Zacharias went out to the woodshed where Patrociño created his famous carvings. He knocked on the ramshackle door but received no answer.

"It's me, Zacharias."

He knocked some more. No answer.

He tried the door. It was latched from the inside. So Zacharias went to the only window, and with his hands on each side of his eyes to block the glare he stared hard through the stained window. His eyes adjusted some to the glass-dimmed light. He could see several beginning carvings on a wooden table.

Then there was a small pile of cedar that he and Indian Tony had brought down from their annual trip to the mountains. He couldn't explain why, but the wood seemed to emanate a feeling of impatience, waiting to feel the carving tools of Patrociño Barela.

There was the ancient chair piled with magazines and old periodicals that Patrociño had showed him so proudly when they had, so often, sipped wine and visited on many subjects. The publications were about the old masters—Van Gogh, Monet, and other masters of their time.

Zacharias remembered how his soft voice softened even more as he spoke of these masters. He did not seem to even dream that he was one of them, but he had to be. Shaw Spencer's best friend, the rico artist Dal Holcomb, said in his very presence that Barela was the most original artist to ever work in New Mexico. That was absolute proof he belonged in the same magazines. Those words had come from the mouth of a man who was paid over forty thousand dollars a year by people in New York who knew everything.

There he was. Patrociño was in a deep sleep on his little couch. It was probably a sleep of exhaustion from all his labors on the cedar. Zacharias started to tap on the window, but then he decided that it might be impolite to awaken one so weary from his labors.

Without being aware of it, he tiptoed away from the frail little studio until he was some yards along on his way back to town. The walk had made him thirsty. As he passed the large house of the late famed Russian artist, Gaspard, he noticed that the yard needed weeds raked. Since he had no money left to quench his thirst after the uphill walk to the Lucky Bar, he had an inspiration—why not inquire if anyone was home, and see about the yard? *Why not, indeed,* Zacharias said to himself. He had a few faults, but being lazy and thoughtless were not among them.

He hesitated, then he knocked on the door. To his surprise the door opened, and the space was mostly filled by a woman.

"I am Zacharias Chacon. I have come to clean the yard of the famous artist Leon Gaspard."

"He is on a tour in New York," she said, with touch of irritation in her voice.

"Si, si. I meant the yard to be cleaned for his next of kin."

"I'm it. I'm the widow."

She looked him over with some care and then said, "Well, come in then, and we'll discuss it."

Zacharias controlled his surprise and entered. "Sit," she said, pointing to a chair.

The large room was full of wondrous things, with paintings on all the walls that both Dal Holcomb and Patrociño Barela would no doubt admire.

He saw her staring at the package for Mama. "Look . . ." he began as he opened one corner. "She has worked these many years for myself and the kids. And now I must get her a present before she is too old to appreciate it."

"That is very thoughtful of you, Zacharias."

"Thank you, Mrs. Gaspard, but you see I have not the money to pay for it. The shop only let me take it for the approval."

The widow said nothing, but she looked steadily at Zacharias. He couldn't tell what she was thinking, but it took a great deal of courage for him to go on. Somehow she looked familiar, but of course he could never have known her.

"Now, if you could let me have five dollars and fifty cents until tomorrow afternoon, I will mow the lawn now and come back and chop the weeds tomorrow."

"Well," she said, "let's drink our coffee and discuss it further."

Suddenly, for no reason he could deduce, Zacharias felt comfortable in Mrs. Gaspard's presence. "Maybe, maybe a touch of cooking brandy would make the coffee more tasty," he ventured.

The suggestion of a smile appeared on Mrs. Gaspard's face. "Ah, an excellent idea," she said, surprising Zacharias with the utterance.

She rose, went to a cabinet of ancient carved doors, and brought out a bottle of cognac. Then she poured a generous splash into Zacharias's coffee and just a touch into hers.

They both smiled. That did it. Zacharias said, "Forgive me, but I knew a girl in high school who smiled just like you. I asked her for a date once, but she turned me down."

"Do you remember her name?"

Zacharias said, "I think her first name was Josey. I don't remember her last."

"Well, I bet I can recall your high school name."

Zacharias was shocked, but he kept his cool and said, unbelievably, "And what was that?"

"Zacky. Zacky Chacon."

He was truly pleased and shocked at the same time.

"Holy Saints—you, you are Josey Ambrose."

"Si, si. Yes, yes. You were a grade ahead of me, Zacky."

They remembered, and now each saw the other as they'd been back then. She fifteen, he sixteen.

Mrs. Gaspard, or Josey Ambrose, now said, almost with glee, "You would never know, but when I heard you won a scholarship to university I regretted not accepting your date request."

They now relaxed and talked of old-school events and friends, like the kids they'd once been. She explained that she'd gone to New York and worked for an art magazine and was assigned a story on a young, promising artist named Leon Gaspard. And that's how they met. He'd joined with her as a journalist, a model, and then a wife. And then suddenly she reverted back from the Taos schoolgirl to the wife, the bookkeeper, and the caretaker of an internationally known artist.

And Zacharias, well, he was a fixer-upper and an all-around handyman.

So he was hired to fix the iron gate in the front yard so it latched correctly and mow the lawn as well as water it afterward. Now he knew he could count on a big weekly job at the Gaspard mansion. Another good day was lived, and Mama's present was secure. "Oh, beautiful world," Zacharias said to his good self.

Later Indian Tony bought him drinks at the Lucky Bar, and Zacharias suddenly decided to whip Indian Tony for stealing Mama's present. The bartender separated them, and after Tony forgave his dear brudder, they got him headed for home. As he crawled into bed beside Mama, he said, "Mama, I did get you a present. Really I did."

Mama said, "Of course, Papa," and she snuggled up next to his already unconscious body and went very happily to sleep. She had been the last thought on his mind before unconsciousness that night. It was a great present that he had left somewhere. Oh well—he would get her an even greater one tomorrow, for his overdue check would most likely come. Vaguely he heard the fire sirens so far, far away.

The next morning and the next day the village of Taos talked about the fire. It was reported in the *Taos News* that Patrociño's wife had said something like, "He turned over a kerosene lamp." Since they had no phone, by the time she was awakened by the light of the flames she could only run to the neighbors for help. The volunteer fire department had arrived to find only the ashes of carvings and would-be carvings, and only a semblance of the beautiful human being.

The wino club spent these days saluting Patrociño for the great man he was. The Lucky Bar extended credit in his honor. The Taos paper had given him a fairly good good-bye; the other major papers of the state gave him three or four inches, and the national papers gave him almost an inch.

Since she had once used some of his carvings to build a fire in the cookstove, many pondered what his wife had to do with his blazing demise. In later mentions in books this was brought up with caution.

For now the friends of Patrociño all had eyes somewhat red.

Mr. Holt at the Taos Inn patted himself on the back with both hands. Over the years he had acquired hundreds of Barela's pieces for a dollar and a half, at the most, and on rare occasions for a bottle of the cheapest wine. Now, soon, they would be worth hundreds each, and erelong it would be thousands.

20

SHAW HAD BEEN WORKING for three days on a portrait of Indian Tony. This was a record of some sort, as Tony only liked to work one day and then be paid. After that it was difficult to get him back on the job. Even a poor portrait of an Indian in a blanket with that romantic, faraway look about him grabbed the tourists. Only one in a hundred knew whether it was good or bad anyway.

Shaw could tell Tony was tiring. Even the supposedly timeless patience of the Indian was slipping away at each stroke of the brush. If he could just keep him a little longer, he could finish it.

"What are you thinking about, Tony?" Shaw asked. He expected no answer, but whenever Tony did answer, no matter what the question, he moved about and grinned in agony.

Tony was thinking about the November just passed, when he and a friend had packed high into Bull of the Woods Mountain country after a deer. He was thinking of how the snow at twelve thousand feet looked like great long rows of white glass and how it shined so that they had to darken under their eyes with soot to keep from going blind. The horse had struggled and breathed frost like peyote smoke out into the pure, pure air. They could look back down thousands of feet and see where the snow was swallowed in the desert. Then, as they dropped down into a draw, they spotted the buck standing a hundred yards away, looking at them from across the indentation. Tony had calmly climbed from his horse, sighted the rifle under the horse's neck so it wouldn't hurt the animal's ears, and shot the buck in the heart.

He was now thinking how delicious the meat had tasted late that night. Especially after the long, hard ride back to the pueblo. His wife had given him more and more until his belly swelled like a snake full of ostrich eggs. It was a happy time even without wine. But a man had to ride a whole day now to find a deer, and maybe not even then.

Tony's answer to Shaw was, "I think of my older brudder, Steaming Prick."

"Steaming Prick?" Shaw said, stopping his brush mid-stroke.

"Yes, he is called that always, on Indian land."

"How in the world did he ever come by a name like that?" Shaw asked with honest interest.

"He do the girl under the hay on cold January day. He see one, two more Indian boys watching. He jump off the girl out from under the wagon, and his prick it steam in January. We laugh like hell all the time about it. He don't mind now. It's a good Indian name on Indian land."

"What's the matter with him, Tony?"

"Oh, he drink too much. Work too little."

Tony shut up for a spell. Shaw almost had the painting. If he could keep him just a minute more.

"Tony, how come you like wine so much?"

Tony talked again. "I like it cause it make me dream good."

"Dream good? Like what?"

Tony was slinging his aching back. "Just dream good, that's all."

Shaw had the painting now. He stepped back and looked at it. He knew he had something for the tourists. It wasn't much, but the color was there, and it was an Indian. It was tourist bait.

He gave Indian Tony ten dollars and thanked him. Tony left after telling Shaw what a good, dear brudder he was twenty-one times. There was a drought going on in Tony that would take a lot of liquid to cure. But a man of his experience could correct this agony in a very short time, especially with a fortune like ten dollars in his pocket. He left.

Indian Tony had it on all the patrons of the Lucky Bar because his ancestors had existed for over nine hundred years in the Taos pueblo. But he didn't care a hoot for these historical facts. His one great desire was to quench a thirst with the blessed grape.

Shaw climbed the scaffold to the huge canvas stretched and glued on the ceiling. He lay on his back and looked at the figures beginning to come out of the maze of color and drawing, all indefinable but coming forth like figures nearing in a fog.

Here, in the canvas wall, he could forget the tourists. Here he painted for Shaw. Here is what he was all about. He picked up the palette and went to work. This precious time was his. He was selfish with it, for it was so seldom that he could work on this, his masterpiece. The brush moved swiftly for a while. He must be inspired by something. He thought of other artists, but that didn't help. Hell, why not Zacharias, his pardner. He never complained. The earth was his dinner and the oceans and rivers his bottle of wine.

He worked on a figure now that looked more and more like Anna. People would come to see it from all over the world, and he would become rich and famous if he ever finished it. He worked on into the night. His neck and arms were full of cramps and felt like a thousand shingle nails had been driven into his bones. He turned on the lights and continued. His muscles pained and pulled more each moment. His eyes burned like a nine-day hangover. But he must go on.

At eleven o'clock his eyes had blurred so that he couldn't tell where to place the next stroke on the great painting. He climbed down stiffly, almost falling from the platform, still holding the brush and palette of paint. He sat, leaning far back, and looked at the picture from a distance. Since it covered the entire ceiling he stretched out flat on the floor.

That is where Zacharias found him later, asleep. He shook him awake, saying, "Pardner, wake up. I have to get Mama a present."

"How much?" Shaw said wearily. "How much?"

"Five dollars and fifty cents."

Shaw arose, his joints howling, and scrounged around in his pockets. He found a five and a one.

"I'll pay you back when I get the check, pardner. I must hurry. It is midnight, and the shops will close soon.

Shaw didn't hear the last, but he went back to sleep on the splintery floor, feeling nothing now.

Zacharias hurried to the Lucky Bar. He wanted to be sure he had a bottle for the morning. He had a strong feeling the check would be here tomorrow. He must be prepared for an early celebration.

21

DIVORCÉE KAY MILLER sat in her black convertible looking exactly like the two million–dollar settlement she'd just received
from her ex-husband. She drove along the twisting road through the
blue sage toward Taos. It was spring. The clear air fairly sparkled and
snapped. In the far mountains to the west one could almost count the
trees, and in the high mountains near Taos one could.

Her red hair gleamed in the sun like a pale ruby, and that same sun
warmed her back where the low-cut, blue dress plunged close to her
hips. She would be forty years old tomorrow, but the hands on the
steering wheel were smooth and graceful. The flesh of her arms was
solid, and the skin of her face was practically flawless, but her large,
blue-gray eyes were hard, and her once full, soft mouth was somewhat
pulled down and drawn.

The woman wasn't happy. In fact, that very morning she'd decided
she was miserable. The two million dollars didn't influence her. She'd
always had money, and if she hadn't, she could have gotten by on her
looks anywhere in the world. Nothing really mattered. Big houses,
filled with antiques and paintings, were taken for granted.

The fact was, she wanted a man—a new one. Of course, getting one
was no problem whatsoever—but which one? She could get a man by
simply walking down the street or stopping in a cocktail lounge. Getting one wasn't the problem. The problem was which one.

Her first husband had been an attorney, bucking hard for a judge-
ship. Her second was a socializing manufacturer of women's garments,
who invaded clubs and prestigious social gatherings with the same dedication Hitler had shown in taking poor Poland. Kay's two sons were
in an eastern boarding school. Except for her maid, she was alone. Oh,
there were the usual little cocktail parties all over the world for those

of wealth or position or beauty, but the thought of another one created a new flood of self-pity.

Just why in hell had the gods given her intellect and beauty supreme when, now, at the peak of her being, she was wasted? If she had the courage she'd shoot herself, she thought. She smiled scornfully, for she was in possession of far too much self-love for that sort of thing. Just the same, she felt low and unneeded and worthless.

She slowed down for a flock of sheep moving across the road. As she braked the long, low convertible to a stop, she pressed impatiently on the horn. Its metallic blast shattered something of quiet and profundity as it vibrated across the serenity of the desert. The sheep neither hurried nor slowed but moved on, each following a leader in a flowing mass of mutton.

Her impatience was unbearable. She pounded the horn again. She wanted to get to town and place her soft wet lips along the rim of a dry martini. The martinis had comforted her more and more of late. But the need grew greater along with the initial blessings.

"Damn it," she swore.

Then she glanced about to see if there was a way she could drive around the flock. There on a slight rise was a man. He was over seventy years old, this man, ragged with a large-brimmed, old hat flopping on his head. A dog stood by his side awaiting instructions. As Kay turned to look at him, he pulled the hat from his head in a great sweep and bowed over his arm to her. As he raised up, a mighty toothless grin ripped a hole in his face.

Suddenly Kay smelled the sage and tasted the pure air of the high country. Her heart pounded just a little, and softness came into her eyes. As the old man passed, she gunned the car down the road, and she too beamed a white, white smile at the old shepherd and waved gaily at him. It was a good world after all in parts, in small ways and hidden places. It was worth living and searching.

On the other side of town Shaw drove his pickup down from the low-slung mesas. He had three more good sketches on his pad and eight dollars in his pocket. He was headed for the Sagebrush Inn for lunch with Dal, who was already sitting at the bar.

"Hi, Dal. How'd your job go?"

"Finished it this morning. We'll go out after lunch and take a look."

Dal had been working on an advertisement for a soap company. Shaw had seen the sketch and could hardly wait to see the finished painting.

"I got in three good sketches this morning. Would you like to see them?"

"Get 'em, boy!"

Shaw walked out to his pickup. As Kay's convertible pulled up to a stop, so did Shaw. He didn't move until she crawled out, flashing white legs and swaying hips, and moved into the bar.

"Class," Shaw said, and he got his drawings.

When he returned he found Kay sitting next to Dal. Gene was mixing her a martini. It was obvious Kay and Dal were acquainted.

She turned to him. "So this is the young artist you've been telling me about?"

"Kay Miller, meet my part-time protégé, Shaw Spencer."

Shaw took her soft hand and shook it like a man's. He felt a little weak around the ankles at first, but he soon found her warm and friendly toward him.

"I'm anxious to see your work," she said. "Dal thinks so highly of it."

"He's prejudiced because I like his mandolin playing," said Shaw.

He and Dal each had a scotch while Kay had two martinis. He noticed how her hand trembled as she raised the first drink, but by the end of the second one she had steadied, and her face was radiant when she said, "Let me see what you have on the sketch pad."

Shaw had been so taken with her beauty he'd forgotten to show the sketches even to Dal.

She looked long and carefully at one—the one where Shaw had tried to sketch the whole of Taos Valley showing the vastness of the sky and the majestic pattern of the clouds.

She finally said, "That's really quite interesting."

"What did I tell you, Kay?" said Dal. "This boy is a real artist."

After lunch Dal invited them to see the painting he'd just done for a soap company. It was a baby sitting in a pan full of suds looking cross-eyed at a huge floating bubble. It was a gem, though Dal put it down as nothing but expert commercialism. As they talked and drank and looked at Dal's other work, Shaw was conscious of Kay watching him every time he looked away. He got up and walked over to a window where he could see her reflection. She was looking right between his shoulder blades as if trying to hear his heart from a distance. He could feel it. Suddenly he whirled and looked her in the eyes. She lowered them gracefully, got up, stretched her willowy figure, and said, "Let's go see some of your originals, Shaw."

He took a bottle of scotch from Dal's larder, and upon entering his studio, Shaw said, "Make yourselves at home. I'll fix us a drink."

Kay took a sweeping glance at the room, at the mural ceiling, at the cumbersome platform that cramped the small studio, and then she concentrated on the individual canvases.

When Shaw returned to the room, Kay was holding up a portrait of Anna. She had also placed three nudes of the same, along with a portrait of Indian Tony, in a row on the floor.

"So, is this the aspiring young artist's favorite model?" she asked.

"It's my most profitable, at least," said Shaw, "because I've sold over thirty paintings of her."

"Would you like to paint me?" she asked.

Dal was getting drunk now, and he said, laughing, "Take her up on it, Shaw, if she'll pose nude."

"Well now," she said. "Why haven't you made the offer yourself, dear Dal?"

"I never had the guts," Dal said.

"Ha," she said, and she turned back to Shaw. "Well?"

"Of course," he said. "When?"

"Tomorrow. I'll commission you."

"For a nude?" he asked.

"No, silly, for a head."

"Oh. Good, tomorrow then."

Dal went to get new drinks so they could celebrate the commission. As he stepped out, Kay said, "You know, I've known Dal Holcomb a long time, and I really like him. He's a fine man, and he's a good artist, but he's always seemed so lost somehow."

"He has plenty of spirit," Shaw said, taking a cue automatically nowadays. "A man is like a painting; his color, his figure, the sound of his voice is of no matter. The question is, does the painting project beyond the confines of the frame? Does the spirit of the man project beyond the body?"

Kay couldn't keep her eyes off the ceiling, but she still hadn't commented about it. After a thoughtful moment she said, "Tomorrow will be a test for us both, won't it?" Then she turned her head at a very attractive angle.

"Hold it," Shaw said. "Don't move!" He walked to her. "That's it. That's the pose I want."

Suddenly he reached out and took her. He felt the bare skin of her back above the low cut of the dress. He kissed her. He didn't paw her or touch her again that day, but late in the evening, when Dal had passed out on Shaw's bed, she put her hand to his face and smoothed the thick auburn hair over his ears and said, "I'm so sorry you're so much younger than I am."

"I can't be," he said. "I'll bet you're just my age."

She started to open her mouth, but Shaw interrupted. "Come on, let's walk down to the Taos Lodge for a drink and let Dal get his nap."

And so he painted the portrait. He made her sit every day for two weeks, although he could have done the painting in a day or two after he finished the sketch. He wanted her to think he was really earning his money. And he left her alone as far as her physical being was concerned until the painting was finished. She stared a lot at this big project on the ceiling, and when she finally asked him about it, he simply shrugged his shoulders. Oddly, he couldn't confide his dream to her.

Then the moment came when they both had to face each other on the canvas. The moment of truth for sure. It was quite a while before Kay commented. Shaw waited, feeling his heart signaling his doubt.

Then she turned to him. "It's a very fine work, Shaw. In fact, it's too good. You did an honest painting. There's no flattery in it."

What she didn't tell him was that he had revealed something to her about herself. Now she knew what afflicted her. It was simply self-pity. It exuded from the canvas. She felt cleansed somehow from seeing her naked face. She walked over, put her arms up around his shoulders, and drew herself to him.

Words would have been wasted, a surplus. The only sounds in the studio were those of physical love.

22

SHAW SPENT MOST of the commission on Kay before the week was out. Martinis come high in Taos, and especially in such a great number, for no matter where they went someone was always joining Kay.

Then, in the middle of the afternoon in Vern Matheny's La Cocina de Taos, on the plaza, he said, "That's all. I'm broke. If you want another drink, you'll have to buy it."

So she slipped him a check for a hundred dollars, and that was it. He knew now that he could depend on her for money as long as things were pleasing her. If not, he wondered what she would do.

She fed him and wined him and ordered two custom-made suits from a tailor in Albuquerque because she didn't appreciate his wearing the old orange sweater everywhere they went.

When he got the suits home and was alone, he traded them to Holt for a crucifix about ten inches high, twenty dollars, and a free drinking spree. After the spree he went to get Anna. They went to a cheap restaurant on the edge of town where they ate his favorite meal, chile rellenos.

The next morning he started another picture of Anna, and he was in the middle of the painting when someone knocked at the door. It irritated him to be bothered, but he answered it anyway. It was the phone-company man.

"I came to connect your phone, Mr. Spencer." He stood holding it in his hand.

"I didn't order a phone," Shaw said.

"Well, I was told to put it in here, so someone must have."

Anna hissed behind his back, "It's your rico girlfriend, seelly."

"Just a minute," Shaw said. He handed Anna a sheet from the unmade bed. "Here, cover yourself. I don't want the telephone company fooling around with you. They control the rest of the world anyway."

The man went to work on the phone, glancing around nervously at Anna, who just stood unmoving with the sheet supposedly covering her. The trouble was, one breast was mostly revealed. The usual efficiency of the man was lowered due to the fact he couldn't keep either his eyes or his mind on his business.

The man had only been gone about five minutes when the new phone rang. Shaw threw the brush on the floor, stomped over, and picked up the receiver.

"Hello," he said brusquely.

"Shaw, darling. I've missed you so. I thought I'd just have your phone put in for you. It's alright, isn't it?"

"No."

"Why, darling, you can have an unlisted number, and no one can call you but me."

He was silent.

"Shaw?"

"Yeah?"

"Are you mad?"

"No, just irritated. I'm busy."

"Can I take you to dinner tonight?"

"I guess so. If I finish this painting."

"What are you painting, darling?"

"Anna," he said, and he hung up.

Anna was prancing out across the room, trying to walk like Kay, holding one finger up as if it was encircled by nine diamonds. Shaw walked over and smacked her on the hind end and said, "Get back on the job, Anna. We're both broke."

"What's the matter, Saw? Did your rico friend take your purse away from you?"

Shaw felt his face burning but went on painting. He didn't speak again until the picture was finished, then he said, "Look, woman, if it wasn't for some of these rich wenches, what would you be doing right now? You'd be down on skid row selling your ass for two dollars today and every day of the week instead of half the time."

Anna said quietly, "I can go now. I don't want to make you feel bad, Saw."

He didn't answer but started to clean up, first the brushes and then himself. While he waited for Kay he studied his new painting. It seemed only seconds before she was there to pick him up.

Without saying anything but, "Hello, darling," she drove out to the edge of town where the sun was setting across the desert. He knew she had something on her mind. He waited. He had more patience than Indian Tony now. It was one of the necessities to survive as an artist.

The shadows across the desert turned so purple they looked as if holes could be punched in them, and the oranges and yellows burst so bright they set the sky aflame.

Then, as grayness gradually came, the nighthawks flew about, snapping their beaks at insects. A great horned owl swished his wings in the stillness, preying, and in a little while, above the distant soft bleating of sheep, came the haunting howl of a coyote.

"Listen to that," Kay said. "I love to hear them howl."

"Me too," Shaw said. "But I wonder how your pleasure at hearing their primeval sounds compares with that of the sheep."

"I wouldn't know since I'm not a sheep. I'm a woman," she said, emphasizing the last word.

"I don't think anyone would deny that."

"I have desires and feelings like other women, Shaw. I want you. I know I'm older," she sped up her speech now, "but I love you just the same. I want to marry you and take care of you. You won't have to hire whores for models anymore, or worry about bills and lawsuits all the time. You can just paint. Just paint all you want, for the rest of your life. I want to give to you. I want to have something worth dedicating myself to. Everyone must have a purpose. You have your ceiling. I at least want a man who has a ceiling to cover."

Shaw reached over and took her hand, and he looked at her in the twilight. He knew she was faking it, but she was doing it with some courage and great skill.

"Well?" she said.

"I'll let you know soon," was all he could say. He couldn't bring himself to tell her he didn't really believe any of it. Shaw truly felt that Kay was lying to herself. She didn't want to give to him. She wanted to take from him. She wanted his company, his body, his talent, to become hers. The money took care of that. And even though she was lying to herself, the benefits to him and his career were surely true. She would have bought all of him. There were a lot of ways for an artist to sell out in this world, a lot of easy, tempting ways. If he wasn't a good artist then he'd really be the fool.

He spent a couple of days trying to figure out what to do. It was a tough proposition to turn down. She had everything. He went down to skid row and got Anna. They sat in a booth and drank the only thing they could afford—cheap wine.

"What bothers you, Saw? You are troubled, no?"

"Yes, I'm troubled," Shaw said. "The rico, corn-headed gringo wench wants to marry me."

Zacharias came over to talk to his pardner. Anna told him in Spanish, "No talk. Play the violin for your pardner. He has a trouble on his heart."

Zacharias picked up the elderly instrument and set his bow. He played. He played so sadly of love that had his pardner been totally free of troubles, his heart would have broken anyway.

Anna said nothing for a moment, then she stood up and said, "For some men that kind of marriage work, Saw, but I theeenk, not for you. You cannot go about like thees," and she put her hand out behind her, palm up.

The two of them got very drunk after that. Zacharias continued to play and smile straight at them. He knew he must play the best of his life. He didn't know why and he didn't care. He just felt good about everything when Shaw danced with Anna. Shaw could smell her sweat, and her hair was stringy, and she was staggering and almost drooling. He took her up the street, across the plaza, and down a back alley to El Patio, where he knew Kay was dining with some of her perpetual friends from the East.

They stumbled into the colorful Mexican restaurant. Shaw asked the headwaiter, who, in fact, owned the place, where Kay was. He pointed into another room. Shaw led Anna along by the hand. She kept pulling back, but she was too drunk to resist much. He guided her up in front of Kay's table and said, "This is Anna, everybody. She's a whore, this Anna. See . . . Look at the poor fool."

He pointed to her face, which was stained around the mouth with wine and had a thin strand of hair stuck in it. "Look at the poor little fool," he said again. "She's not only a two-dollar whore, but she's a wino and a petty thief to boot. But she bought my wine tonight from money she made in an alley on the cold, hard ground, and she'll go sleep with me now for nothing, and then again tomorrow she'll pose for me. Tonight I'm drunk. Tomorrow I'm an artist, and a man. My *own* man." Shaw felt that his words and actions were crazy, stupid, but it mattered little. He suddenly felt aware. Vibrant. With that he left the table before they could ask the manager to evict him. He dragged Anna out into the alley with his arm around her waist, singing loudly something with no tune as he stumbled toward his home. And that is how Shaw Spencer said no and good-bye to the marriage proposal of Kay Miller.

Near the end of the alley, Shaw stopped singing and started talking. Anna stood swaying in the moonlight, listening, not understanding a word of it.

"I want to think every thought there is to think," he shouted. "I want to make love to every woman alive and drink all the wine in the world. I want to feel all the pain, the pleasure, the love, the hate, the humor, the idiocy, and the suddenness of all mankind right here!" He pounded himself violently on the chest. "I want to climb the highest mountain, and with a pine tree in each hand I want to beat the world like a drum. Do you hear me, Anna? Do you hear?"

She nodded her head yes. She did hear, and she didn't need to understand. Whatever Shaw said was the true gospel.

"And that's not all. That's only the beginning. I want to paint, yes, paint in glorious and moving colors, all these things a thousandfold. All of them on my ceiling."

He leaped into the air, shouting at the sky of transparent blue lead with a three-quarter starter moon hanging half in fear.

He fell. Anna tried to pick him up. She fell. He pushed her away and staggered upright. He tried to get her up. She was motionless to his urging. He finally struggled her into a sitting position. Then, with a tendon-tearing effort, he got her half over his shoulder. With the dead weight and the wine, his heart pumped hard to his brain and set him to stumbling again. Anna was slipping off, and he lunged forward, trying to get under her body again before the tops of both their heads struck a garage door. Anna didn't feel it at all when Shaw dropped her face up, arms and legs spread wide, but he did. He rambled around holding his head on until the lightning and thunder quit flashing and roaring between his ears. He had learned a lesson this last moment.

He took Anna's arms and dragged her around the garage into some tall weeds. He looked around for something to cover her with. Across the alley he spotted some large cardboard boxes in a wood container. He took one and placed it over Anna. Her face and body were covered, but her feet stuck out. He made an adjustment, but now her head was uncovered, and the edge of the box was choking her. He finally pushed all of her under the box, then he crawled about on his knees until his hand touched a large rock. He raised it up and, reeling somewhat, placed the rock on the box. He was very pleased with himself as he walked away, saying, "Good night, darling Anna."

He'd forgotten Anna by the time he arrived home, but something stirred in him yet besides wine. He looked at his ceiling and knew he'd never be able to climb the platform tonight, so he took a sketch pad and wrote a poem of sorts.

I'm drunk
I'm drunk with wine
Soon I'll be fine
No more words
this time.

He fell asleep on top of the covers. The Taos night was calm now.

23

"MAMA, COME HELP ME PUSH SEÑOR BUICK," Zacharias yelled. "I must go to town for business."

Mama put down the iron, pushed the hair from her sweating face, and went out to help him push. It was no problem, since they were parked on a hill. As soon as the car started moving Zacharias jumped in, put it in gear, and pushed the foot pedal. It stuttered, jerked a moment, and then the motor clanked into action. Zacharias stopped and raced the motor. Smoke exuded in a choking cloud from the exhaust. The car shook and trembled like a frightened elephant for a few seconds, then it settled down to a fairly steady purr. It could start all day now that it had been well warmed.

It was Saturday, and much business must be taken care of. First he would look up his son Romo. It was late fall, and shoe shining would not be so good as in the summer. Besides, Romo dodged him all the time on Saturday because he didn't want to miss the first picture show. He knew if Zacharias found him before he got into the movie house he would take away his money.

Romo was so big now it embarrassed him to be carrying a shine box around. He was talking to a smaller boy, a son of a grocer who had some money in his pocket. He tried to use a small part of his father's orating on the kid. He told him, "You know, Carlos, I might sell you this shoe shine business if you had enough money."

"Why?"

"I'm going to work in the mines next year. I won't be able to run this business."

"The mines are closed."

"They are going to open soon. The *Taos News* says so."

"You are too young to work, even if the mines do open."

"That is to be seen. My father, Zacharias, is a bulldozer operator, and he will have a big contract from the mines as soon as he gets his check."

"What check?"

"The government owes him. Thousands of dollars. He and Mr. Spencer are going into business together. They will surely hire me."

Romo studied Carlos as he figured his father would do. Carlos picked his nose and scratched his eight-year-old butt with the other hand. He looked off across the street at the picture show.

"Well, I'm going to the show now."

Romo was thinking fast. "Last summer I shined five dollars' worth on one Saturday. One. Do you hear, Carlos?"

Carlos heard. He pushed his hands deep into his pockets. "In one day?"

"Of course. And also, in one week I made seven dollars and twenty cents."

"But . . . it is not summer now."

"Haaaww . . . What does that matter? Soon the skiers will be here. They all want shines!" Romo lied as he felt his father would do. Skiers never wanted shines at all, but it was the best story he could think of.

"They do?"

"You can charge them double for ski boots. They stand in line."

"They do?"

"You can make a fortune between now and summer. Think of what you can do next summer."

"How much for the business?"

"How much you got?"

"Five dollars that Uncle Felix gave me for Christmas."

"That's not enough," said Romo, his heart feeling like an alarm clock going off in a cold room.

"I'll give you five dollars and a candy bar every day for a month."

"How will you get the candy bar?"

"My father has a grocery, you know."

"That's right. Okay, Carlos, you are stealing this from me, but it's a deal. You can have the shine box, all the polish, the rags, and the brush. That must be worth twenty dollars, not counting all my regular customers."

Carlos stuck one finger back in his nose. The other hand came out of the pocket with five one-dollar bills in it. Romo grabbed them before the sun touched them, dropped the twenty-dollar shine box, and turned to run toward the picture show.

Something held him. Some force. It was Zacharias pulling him to the side and behind a shrub.

"What do you mean selling out our business without consulting your pardner? Don't I make the box for you?"

"Yes."

"Didn't I finance your first polish?" Zacharias waited a moment. "Well, didn't I?"

"Yessss," he agreed with difficulty. It would do no good to argue that the money had come from Mama's ironing.

"How much money do you have there?"

"A little."

He took it out of Romo's pocket. He turned Romo loose while he counted it.

"Here's your half," he said, holding two dollars out in one hand. As Romo reached for it, Zacharias took one of the bills back. "I'll keep this for you," he said with fatherly kindness. "It's too much money for a young boy to carry around. Someone might rob you, and your papa wouldn't want to be responsible for that."

Romo took his dollar and ran as hard as he could to the line in front of the theater.

Zacharias walked across the plaza, got into his car, and drove to the Conoco Station on the corner of the plaza. He purchased two dollars' worth of gas from Jimmy Farrell and drove happily around to skid row.

The bartender knew Zacharias so well that he just set out a glass of wine. Zacharias smiled and beamed like a young man who had just conquered a long-sought-after virgin. Like the Lover at only the sight of a new female challenge. Like the Undertaker with a fresh corpse. Like the Woodhauler at a barn full of cut piñon. Like Indian Tony at a full bottle with the cork removed. Like Shaw Spencer at a successful nude painting of Anna. Like Mama at a stack of freshly ironed shirts.

"Give me two bottles of Tokay."

"Two?"

"Can't you hear today, my amigo?" And Zacharias held up the index finger on both hands and moved them together.

The Undertaker came in and sat down by Zacharias. He was quiet. Waiting. His hands shook, and his tongue felt dry as a lizard's back. He needed a drink badly. He stared at the paper sack with the distinct shape of two wine bottles on the bar near Zacharias. His eyes glazed over like those of the dead. Finally he raised his head. His nostrils flared, and his trembling condition was gone for moment.

"Look!" He pointed through the window. "Hans Paap, the Iron One!"

"What about it?"

"Haven't you noticed? Are you blind, Zacharias?"

"What is it?"

"You don't see? Oh, you are in trouble if you have become so unseeing. Look, he can only take two consecutive steps instead of three. It takes him two-thirds of the day now to walk to town.

"No matter, he has been a great man," said Zacharias. "They say he once hit a steer with his fist and killed it like a butchered lamb. They say he once rode twenty broncos to a standstill in one day. They say he made love to more women in a year than the Lover has in all his life."

"You speak of the devil. Yes, here he comes."

They watched as the Lover stopped a moment and talked to the old man. If the Iron One heard he made no sign. Perhaps all was beneath him.

The Lover came in.

"What did he say?" asked the Undertaker.

"He said that only I could surpass his abilities with women."

"You lie," said Zacharias. "He would never admit such a thing, even to you."

"True," said the Undertaker.

"He is a great man. A great man," said Zacharias.

"All the more thrill at his fall. Look," the Undertaker said gleefully, "he even tottered on his first step that time. I shall watch him closely every day of this winter. Some cloudy, snowy day he'll freeze, and I'll find him. It is my privilege."

Zacharias said to the Lover, "Did you go to the mail?"

"Of course, papa-in-law. Nothing."

"Soon," said Zacharias. He could no longer send Rosita every day, for she had the young one at home now and another one in her belly. So she sent her idle husband instead—for a letter that seemed to be lost in the mail.

"Come, let's go for a ride," Zacharias said. They followed, eagerly watching the paper sack. Indian Tony joined the procession without comment. He knew.

Señor Buick failed to start, but at the last faltering second fire ignited gasoline and they drove away. The group circled the plaza feeling very important, and then they drove down below the La Tuatah Court, where there was a vacant lot and a single cottonwood tree of smooth dimensions. In the summer this tree gave shade and a place to hide a bottle. Thousands of pieces of broken glass sparkled in the bright winter sun. They stopped near the barren tree out of habit and love for its great bulk. It was a tree of heart. It gave much and received little. But then it needed little. There was a small swamp just below it, and the roots easily reached to water.

The first bottle was passed. Trembling hands and eager lips were pacified.

"It's a good day," said Zacharias, feeling the steering wheel almost lovingly, like he felt Mama's butt.

"All days are good," said the Lover. "Someone is making love somewhere at any moment in time. Is that not enough to make good days?"

"Someone is dying at any given moment, too," said the Undertaker, smiling and half closing his eyes so as to dream better of death.

Tony said, "This good day, brudders. Good." And he took himself another big swallow of wine.

"I had another letter from the Veteran's Company last week," said Zacharias.

"You mean from the Veteran's Administration," corrected his informed son-in-law.

"That's the name," Zacharias agreed. "The Veteran's Company said they would soon have my money. I'm going to buy you and Rosita a new TV set and an extra bed for the new baby. And for Mama," he said, throwing his arms apart, "I shall buy Mama a new world bigger and rounder than this one. She can play with it like a baby shakes a rattle."

"What shall you do for me?" asked the Undertaker.

Indian Tony, polite as always, said, "Thank you, dear brudder. Dear brudder—I thank you for . . . for . . . for bein' here."

"You know. I've always told you I'd buy you a funeral of your own, where you're in complete charge of all the details. And then, of course, I have to get Juandias, the Woodhauler, five hundred bottles of wine."

"We help him drink it, brudder?" asked Tony.

"Of course. He will need our help, and we must not let him down."

"He's our friend," said the Lover.

"That is right," said Zacharias. "And of course you all know that my true and loyal friend, Shaw, will have a percentage of the large profits I make from my bulldozer."

"Surely," said the Undertaker.

"It will be a great day, brudders," said Tony. "Like this day, brudders." Taking a final swallow, he rolled down the window and threw the empty bottle against the tree. It broke, losing its pieces among the thousands of other broken dreams scattered about.

"Look," said the Undertaker, pointing down the road. "Matias, the Fighter!"

The Fighter came down the road, weaving and stumbling back and forth. He would take several steps forward swiftly, and then, before he fell, he'd stop and take two or three backward. He covered over a mile walking three blocks.

The Undertaker cried with elation, "Look, he got beat up!" The cut on his forehead was streaming blood. He put his dirty coat sleeve to his head to sop it up. They let him into the back seat where he sat, still holding his arm on his head and snorting through his fractured nose. It didn't really matter that he couldn't see without prizing his eye apart.

Most of his thoughts and sights were turned inward, anyway, and had been for years.

Soon now the second bottle was empty. No one had any money to buy more.

Zacharias said, "My dear son-in-law, I would like to ask you a favor, not for myself, but for us all."

The Lover looked at him with some suspicion on his face as Zacharias continued. "I know that you are true to my Rosita most of the time. I also know that you had a friendship with Emilia at the restaurant where you received many favors. You could still, I'm sure, convince her that we need two more bottles of wine."

"Impossible—I haven't seen her for months. Not since my wedding vows with your daughter and my beloved wife, Rosita."

"Ah, I realize your faithfulness, and Mama and I appreciate it. The only thing is, I wouldn't want Rosita to know that I saw you go in the back door of the restaurant the other evening on my way home."

"It was only to get a hamburger."

"She must make them in her bedroom then, for I drove around the block and back in front of the restaurant, and it was as dark as the inside of a shoebox."

"I'll see what I can do," said the Lover, and he departed.

"A fine son-in-law," said the Undertaker.

"That is right. A fine boy. You can depend on that boy."

"He is our best brudder," said Tony, pulling his blanket tight against the chill.

It took the Lover some time to get the money. Emilia closed the restaurant while they retired to the back. The Lover had to apply bedroom psychology to high finance to accomplish the mission. As he left the bed she handed him a dollar and sixty-five cents.

On his return he was greeted by many shouts of congratulations. One more bottle was emptied. The sun was creeping low in the west, and the cold came sneaking back across the valley to take over from the red master in the sky.

"We shall drive," said Zacharias. "That way we can turn on the heater without running the battery down."

He stepped on the starter. It went *err . . . err . . . errrr.* But the car would not start. He tried again. Then there was a final tiny *err,* and then nothing.

"We'll have to push Señor Buick," Zacharias said. "Get out and push."

He stayed in the car to drive. There wasn't enough strength in the entire group to completely turn the wheels over. The best they could do was sort of rock it back and forth like a crib.

"Tony, go get my pardner, Shaw. Go tell him to come and pull this car."

"I go," said Tony. "Give one little drink, keep this Indian warm."

Zacharias held on to the bottle and quickly took it away from Tony's lips. "Now go."

It was getting colder and colder in spite of the insulation of the wine. It was almost dark when Tony came back with Shaw. He had had a difficult time getting Shaw to answer the door. In fact, Shaw had been on a drinking party—a farewell party for Dal Holcomb. The world had finally come around and knocked on Dal's door and said, "You can't work out here and make a living. You've got to come back east and work under heavy hands so we can squeeze and mash you into our shape." Dal had no choice. He'd been at it too long to change his life's work. He had to leave the land he loved. It saddened Shaw, and whenever he'd been sad he had bad hangovers.

When he and Tony arrived at the trouble spot, he removed a chain from under the pickup seat. It was all he could do to stand the cold until he got the chain attached to Señor Buick. Zacharias gave him a drink of wine, and then he felt better. Off they went.

Up on the Loma, down by the schoolhouse, then northwest toward Questa highway. The car stubbornly refused to start.

Shaw turned on the main highway where he could get more speed. They all strained forward, trying to help with feelings alone, gritting their teeth, clenching and tightening their shaking muscles.

"Pool, pool," yelled Zacharias, forgetting a moment his formal speech. "Pool the son of a beech."

Zacharias thought that if you pulled long enough, and fast enough, it would start. And if it started, all you had to do was drive it long enough, and it would repair itself, no matter what was wrong with it.

"Pool, pool, pool faster!" They were all yelling now, figuring any encouragement would help.

And sure enough it finally started. Faith. Pure faith.

They drove down the street to where Shaw lived. Just after turning the corner, Zacharias rammed his car into the back of the pickup. A few things were bent, but nothing that ran or turned. Shaw didn't care. The finance company was taking it away from him next week anyway if he didn't make another payment.

After parking the pickup and replacing the chain under the seat, he joined the others in the car. They drank the wine and talked of many worldly things.

Then, in a moment of sentimentality, Zacharias decided to drive to Ranchos and show his pardner Shaw the house where he was born and the creek from which he carried thousands of gallons of water. There was just one thing wrong. Ranchos was south, and they pulled out on the highway in front of the Taos Lodge heading north. There would have been some doubt as to whether the old car would have held up long enough for them to reach Ranchos if they had been going in the right direction, but as it was it didn't matter. In front of the Kachina Lodge, where the road curved to the west, Zacharias waved a bottle in the air with one hand while emphasizing the point of a story with the other. Señor Buick, being barely able to run with all the help it could get, could do nothing whatsoever about steering itself alone. It whizzed right out over the corner post of the Sierra Vista Cemetery, cracking the post in half as well as the front bumper, finishing off the grill, and knocking a hole in the radiator with one smash.

The Undertaker was running around the car, shouting, "Look, Look! The graves are so beautiful by car light. Zacharias, you have warmed my heart! I shall have a deep respect and love for you always." He bent down and tried to read the inscription on a marker.

"This is old Moses Martinez," he cried. "I knew him when I was a boy. A rattlesnake bit him. He died in beautiful agony."

The Undertaker said profoundly, "God is gravity. He has taken our car."

"Shut up, you ghoul, and help push," said Shaw.

Finally Shaw and the Lover grabbed him by each arm and dragged him behind Señor Buick.

The Undertaker quivered in joy and said, "Look! The lights have gone! Now the ghosts will rise!"

"Any ghost that would come out on a night like this deserves to be dead," said the Lover.

Then they heard it—the siren!

They ran out from the graveyard, stumbling over hundred-year-old tombstones and falling into crosses and little plots with fences and dried flowers.

The spotlight came searching, but they hid in the weeds and hugged the frozen ground. They could hear the police as they examined the car. "It belongs to Zacharias Chacon. We'll get him in the morning. Here, help me with this one," and they pulled the Fighter from the back seat, where he'd innocently slept through it all.

They were almost frozen now. With much stiffness they arose and sneaked through the night, hiding and dodging all sights, lights, and sounds until they arrived at Shaw's studio. There they slept, some on the bed, some beside it, and Indian Tony under it. Tony, believe it or not, liked to be alone on occasion. This was the occasion.

It took all morning for them to rake up enough money for Zacharias to face the judge. The Fighter had simply been fined ten dollars for drunkenness and released.

"What do you mean driving into to a graveyard and desecrating hallowed ground?" the judge said in Spanish to Zacharias.

"We were there to simply honor our amigo, the Undertaker."

The judge, perhaps fifty-five years old, five feet tall, and a cigar chewer of the utmost dedication, spit out around the cigar with an unbelieving sound and said, "Geelty? Not Geelty?"

"Judge, I tell you . . ."

"Geelty? Not Geelty?"

It really didn't matter what Zacharias said or did. It didn't matter if he was innocent or not, no one had ever been found innocent by this justice of the peace officer. Ever. And they never would, because he got half the money from fines, so he fined everyone the limit the law allowed.

"Guilty," Zacharias said, sighing and reaching for the money his friends had raised with such difficulty.

As he walked out into the street, he was glad that he had enough left to buy a bottle of wine, and he was happy he escaped spending a night in the Taos dungeon.

24

THE BUNCH OF THEM lolled about the Resting Place. All were afoot now. The night just passed had been one of the year's coldest, but they were reasonably comfortable here in the sun and out of the wind. Their breaths fogged out in little jets of steam as they hunkered up in their coats. Each seemed to be deep in thought, trying to concentrate on anything but the cold.

Shaw broke the silence. "Some zillion or so years ago our ancestors crawled out of the sea on their bellies. Then they stood upright. Later they returned to the top of the sea in boats, and the bottom in submarines, and finally came the wheel. Then they tried to be birds and fly around in planes and rockets. Man wants to be everything—except for man, it would appear."

This aroused something in Zacharias. "Last night I had a dream," he said. "It was a dream of great strangeness, even more so because it might come true." He took his glasses off and cleaned them on the sleeve of his coat. He touched the tiny rim of his gray hat tenderly, as if it might fall apart—which indeed it might have with the slightest abuse.

"I dreamed," he went on, sensing he'd captured his audience, "that I owned twenty-five bulldozers. I lined them up, with twenty-five drivers and myself, on the mountains to the east of town. I, Zacharias, was the general in command. I stood on my dozer and shouted, 'Charge,' and down the mountains we rolled, gaining momentum at every turn of the wheels. We proceeded to sweep Taos into a great pile of adobe, businessmen, writers, artists, and other such uselessness. Then we moved west and shoved the whole mess into the Rio Grande Gorge. This created a mighty dam, and it backed the river up for miles, forming a lovely blue lake. Trees, bushes, and grass sprouted all along its banks. Wildlife of all sorts came to play and live along its shores. Oh, my amigos, it was a sight to dream about."

There was appreciation in all the worn faces.

The Lover spoke now, his eyes showing much life. "Dear father of my wife, you've given me a dream this moment. I will build a bright aluminum building fifty-two stories tall where Taos once was."

"Aluminum?" said the Undertaker, disapproving of the brightness, for he loved only darkness.

"Yes, aluminum, so the world can see and envy this place of joy." Now the Lover's imagination sailed through the clear air in soaring circles and curves. "You see, I shall have many beautiful women on each floor, of different nationalities, colors, and constructions. I, Flavio Bernal, the Champion Lover of Taos, will spend a week on each floor. This way I can love my way up one year and love my way back down the next. Fifty-two floors of wonderful women." He finished, dreaming to himself.

Shaw, the once fresh-faced young artist, stood up and beat the Lover on the back. "I'll go along and paint a nude of the most beautiful one on each floor."

Zacharias, realizing he'd been outdone for once by his son-in-law, immediately changed the subject. "Did you hear about the Iron One last night?"

The Undertaker whirled, and some resemblance of life came across his ever-yellowing features. "What, Zacharias? What? Did he get run over? A stroke, perhaps?"

"No, worse than that. He was found standing up, frozen to death in the alley by the Harwood Foundation. He was stiffer than an iron post."

There was utterance of sadness and regret from some, but the Undertaker moaned and grabbed his homely face.

"Oh God," he cried. "My dream—why couldn't I have found him? I've waited for years. Eternities! How could he do this to me?" He butted his head against the adobe wall of the liquor store.

Zacharias, seeing that the Undertaker was in a bad way, reached out and grabbed him by the shoulders then turned him toward a couple of older men walking along the edge of the street.

"Guess," he said.

They had just recently started playing the "guessing game" when the wine was in short supply and things became desperate. This morning only one pint had been passed around.

The Undertaker said, clearing his voice, "They're artists."

"No," said Shaw. "The one on the left is a writer. The only thing worse than a painter is a writer."

They all studied the two men carefully. One was close to seven feet tall, bent like a rusty wire, bearded, and dressed all in grays and dirty. The other was the same except he was short and had a slight protruding belly. His hands hung from his sleeves like a chimpanzee's. He dragged his feet, and he was also filthy.

All agreed Shaw was right. Shaw was an artist and therefore had that advantage of judgment about his own kind.

Later a couple of tourists strolled along with cameras. The man was big and wore a knit cap over a florid face. His wife was big, too, and had on a red, woolly pair of stockings of the same material and color as her husband's cap.

The Lover spoke. "He is one of those men who dig."

"Dig what?" asked Zacharias, craving to relegate his son-in-law to his proper position.

"You know, old bones, giraffes, dinosaurs, that sort of thing."

"And what about the woman?" said Zacharias.

"She does the same. She keeps the records and sees that he never strays from his duties."

"That shows how little you know of life, Lover. Notice the fat of the huge stomach on both. Could they bend and pick bones all day? No, of course not. They are the desk type. The man is principal in one of those rich men's schools, and his wife only teaches the subject you just mentioned."

"An archaeologist," Shaw helped.

"That's right," said Zacharias. "Archaeologists." Zacharias was voted the winner of this go around. Now it was Indian Tony's turn as two swaggering young men dressed like cowboys moved along.

"No cowboys," said Tony. "Maybe sheeps men."

"No, Tony, old brave," said Shaw. "Those men work for the telephone company. All their hired hands dress like cowboys in New Mexico. The Bell Telephone Company has more cowboys employed than there are members in the Rodeo Cowboy's Association."

"Sheeps men," insisted Tony.

Shaw was declared the victor again, although the Lover voted it a draw.

A lone figure of a man walked by with his head down. He was of average height with thin hair and thick glasses over a thin nose and mouth.

"Bookkeeper," Zacharias said.

There was full agreement on this one. And on and on it went, for they had nothing better to do. But soon Shaw tired of the game. He was trying to think. He was broke. He was afoot. In his house there stood an easel without a canvas, a palette without paint, a floor without a model, a cupboard without food. A canvas-covered ceiling with no artist to work on it. There was a cover on his bed, but this was of little comfort when his stomach chewed and growled with hunger.

He got up and looked around helplessly at his amigos. Then he made a decision. He would go to Anna's house. If she hadn't shacked up somewhere the night before, she would be home. It was too early for her to inhabit the bars.

Zacharias decided, since he was the unquestionable leader, to drive them all to their home-away-from-home in Señor Buick. However, Señor Buick seemed to have an independent mind of his own. He was as silent and unmoving as a gravestone.

The Undertaker said, "Señor Buick is testing our patience before he sparks to life. Señor Buick is happiest when dead, as we all are."

The group from the Resting Place were all there, and they all took turns looking under the hood, kicking the thin tires, touching Señor Buick here and there on its body where the paint had vanished. There was muttering with unknown tongues, all to coax the old iron beast into starting. At last Señor Buick grew weary of toying with all the experts. He cleared his throat, coughed, sputtered, and shook all over until the sparks touched the gasoline and he stuttered into life. All were soon aboard—or rather in—the old auto. Zacharias, like the chauffer for an emperor, drove the wine-loving crew proudly around the historic Taos Plaza and then back down the highway to Santa Fe, to the Sleeping Boy Bar, then he turned back toward the Taos Plaza and parked perfectly in the very front of home—the Lucky Bar.

25

SHAW WOUND AROUND THE ALLEY to the little adobe. He knocked on the door and an old toothless woman, Anna's mother, opened it. She recognized him and said in Spanish, "Enter."

Anna was bent over a pan, washing her hair. She looked out from under it, trying to keep the soap out of her eyes.

"Saw," she smiled, "in a minute."

The old woman, bent and stiff from arthritis but with eyes black and shining as obsidian, motioned to a sofa. Two small children came from another room. Twisting their grandmother's skirt, they stared at him in big-eyed silence.

"Come here," Shaw said to the little girl who looked about six. Anna said something in Spanish.

The little girl came forward, hesitantly at first, and then she ran, jumped onto his lap, and looked up at him.

"See?" she said, and she opened her hand. There was a little silver cross in it.

"Oh, that's very pretty," Shaw said. "Where did you find it?"

Isabel just went on looking up at him with immense brown eyes.

"Where did you get it?" he repeated.

She turned and pointed to her grandmother.

"That's mighty nice," Shaw said.

Anna's eight-year-old son came nearer and leaned on the table. "I have twenty-eight cents," he said. "I earned it sweeping the store."

"What store, Manuel?"

"The grocery store."

"Saud's grocery store on the Santa Fe highway?"

He nodded yes.

"What are you going to buy with all that money?"

"Candy."

"With all of it?"

"Si, I'm hungry for candy."

"He's hungry for everything," said Anna.

"Okay, vamos," she said to the kids as she wrapped a towel around her head and sat down next to Shaw.

The kids did as they were told and went back into the other room. The old woman sat in a wooden rocker by the potbellied stove and started sewing on a dress she was making for Isabel.

"You got any money?" Shaw asked softly.

"No," Anna said and shook her head. "We got the welfare check, but it was quick all gone for wood and groceries."

"Well, I hated to bother you, Anna, but I've hocked everything loose. I don't have a single canvas to peddle nor one to paint, except for the ceiling, of course, and you know I can't sell it. I must exhibit that all over the world."

"Of course. I'm sorry, Saw," she said.

"Oh, it's not your worry. It's just a fact that if I had the supplies I could make us both some money."

"Look," she said, "it is my time of the month. I can't turn a trick for two days. Then I help."

"No, don't worry. I'll pull something before the day is over."

He got up to leave and told the old woman, "Adios, señorita." And he yelled at the kids to behave and not eat too much candy.

He went up to the Taos Inn. He stopped at the desk and talked to Holt a minute as he examined the bar. He could see only one lone figure of a man sitting at a table near the bar.

Holt asked, "How are things going?" But he knew very well how they were going. He'd seen too much. He'd set too many traps for small game such as Shaw Spencer. He knew.

"Fine," said Shaw. "Just fine," and he walked slowly into the bar. He was halfway there when he heard his name.

"Shaw! Shaw Spencer!"

He turned to look. In the corner, at a table, sat Kay Miller and a man.

"Come here, Shaw. I want you to meet my husband, Arthur Mansfield."

Shaw walked over. A heavy, muscled figure with a beard and a face like a Neanderthal rose and took his hand, crushing it painfully.

"Glad to meet you," Shaw said.

"Same here," said the bearded man. "Won't you take a chair?"

Shaw did, and after a moment Arthur continued, "I like the portrait you did of Kay. It has character."

"That's really a compliment, Shaw. Arthur here paints in abstract. He seldom likes the work of a realist."

"I'm not a realist," Shaw said bluntly.

"What then?" Arthur asked.

"I'm a feeler. I paint a recognizable subject with feeling and emotion. It's that simple."

"Let's not talk painting psychology now," said Kay. "I want to know how your career is going."

"Fine," Shaw said, "just fine."

"Where are you showing now?"

"I'm not. I'm on vacation."

"You can't mean that," she said, laughing uncertainly.

"Yeah. I'm tired of painting. Thought I'd quit for a while."

"You can never tell whether he means it or not," Kay said to her husband. "You know, I almost married Shaw once."

Mansfield sort of stiffened and tensed his mighty muscles.

Shaw looked at Kay and said, "When did you get back from Europe? I haven't seen you in over a year."

"Last week. It's good to be back."

"*My God*," Shaw said under his breath. The woman had really gone to hell since he'd last seen her. The hand that held the martini was shaking so bad it slopped the drink out on the bar table. The fingers that held the cigarette were quivering and yellowed from nicotine. Her skin was like wet, brown paper, and the bags drooping under her eyes glistened with cream where she'd tried to smooth them. Her cheeks sagged, and there was a thin surplus of skin hanging down under her chin and neck. Her lips still looked the same, except that she was constantly chewing and twisting them about.

Well, she'd found her artist. She'd gotten what she thought she wanted. At least he was getting fat on it. But he was also getting mean. The look that projected from his whole being said plainly, "I'LL SMASH ANY THOUGHT THAT GETS IN MY WAY. I'LL DESTROY ANYONE WHO ALTERS MY PATH TO KAY'S CHECKBOOK."

Kay said, "Like a drink?"

"No, I'm not drinking today," he lied, his belly contracting at the thought of a cool beer or warm wine.

He put his arm casually over some change lying on the table. In a moment he dragged it off with a smooth gesture. His legs were closed, and he felt the change hit his lap. It was risky. If Arthur had seen him do it he'd have used his muscles on him for sure. Neither noticed.

Kay went on with her small talk and ordered more martinis. Then suddenly she leaned over. She looked Shaw over with regret and said to her almost new husband, "Shaw thinks he's the reincarnation of Michelangelo. Isn't that right, Shaw?"

He avoided the question, knowing trouble would follow her line of thought. She'd never let up now.

Shaw reached slowly into his lap, felt three coins, and clasped them tightly in his hand. He stood up, saying, "It was good to meet you, Art, and it was nice seeing you again, Kay." And he walked toward the bar.

"Beer," he said to Jo, hoping he'd taken enough change. Then he looked. He had three quarters. Well, he was good for two beers now. He felt better. He was out of cigarettes, so he reached and took three out of Jo's pack while she bent over to get the beer.

He heard a fussing noise in Kay's corner, a shuffling of chairs and footsteps leading two uncertain people out of the bar.

Without allowing the foam to settle, he took several healthy swallows of beer. It was cold all the way down. After relishing the taste a moment, he lit a cigarette and turned on the stool. That's when he felt the man sitting there. He felt him before he saw him.

The man was about six feet tall, of average build, with thinning and tight, curly, gray hair. He had a narrow, sagging face and tired gray eyes. He held a whiskey and soda tightly as if he'd like to break the glass in his hand until there was nothing but powder.

Shaw did something he had never done before. He went over to the man and said, "Can I join you for a drink?"

The man seemed startled. "Yes. Yes, of course."

"Here's to the gods," said Shaw, raising his beer.

"The best," the man said, lifting his drink just off the tabletop. "You live here?"

"Yes," Shaw said. "I'm an artist. Well, at least I'm trying to be one." Then he saved the man the next question. "My name is Shaw Spencer."

"Glad to know you," the man said, sticking a cold, tight hand into Shaw's without giving his own name. "An artist," he said, staring at the top of the table. "An artist. What's it like to be an artist?"

"I don't know how to tell you that—only an artist knows he can never make it clear. It just possesses you like drink," he said, raising his beer.

"You mean it's an addiction?"

"I think so. I think the chemistry of some people is such that they must have creation in order to live. I guess kinda like a diabetic needs insulin."

"I never would have thought of it that way," the man said, drumming his fingers rapidly on the table.

"Well, that's only what I think," said Shaw. "That doesn't matter much. Other people feel differently no doubt."

"I'd like to see your work," said the man.

"I'm out. I'm sold out," Shaw said.

"When will you have some more?"

"I don't know. It depends."

"On what?"

"When I get to work."

"Oh, do you have to be in the mood? That sort of thing?"

"Well, that's part of it. There's lots else." Shaw could never remember a single time when he'd had the supplies that he wasn't in the mood. Not one.

Shaw and the man talked and talked. It was strange, he felt, that the man said nothing about himself. Usually when he met those travelers here, they talked altogether of themselves and of personal things after their usual preliminary questions about his work. They told of wives, of jobs, of hatreds and loves. They told of frustrations and inferiority complexes, and then they'd get drunk and brag on everything they had done or would do. This was off the pattern, and so was he.

Suddenly the man said, "Excuse me. I'll be back in a minute."

Shaw sat drinking the whiskey the man had bought him, pondering.

He was gone ten or fifteen minutes, and then he returned and hurriedly sat down. "I'm sorry," he said, "I had to see someone." Then he leaned across the table. "Something is bothering you, isn't it?"

"Yes," Shaw admitted.

"Would you like to talk about it?"

"No, it's only my problem," Shaw said.

"Here. I want you to do me a favor, and take this." He stretched across the table and stuck something in Shaw's shirt pocket.

Shaw started to protest.

"Please."

Something in the voice of urgency stopped Shaw and he said, "All right."

"Waitress, bring us two more," he said. Then he turned to Shaw and said, "You don't know it, but you saved my life this afternoon. I was going to kill myself."

Shaw didn't ask why. It would have been an infringement. After the drink he went to the restroom and looked in his pocket. He found a folded hundred-dollar bill in it. He was astounded. He hurried back to the bar. The man was gone.

"Jo, where did that man go?"

"He didn't say anything to me. He just simply left."

Shaw turned and walked as fast as possible to the Laughing Lady's store. He bought paints and canvas. He went across the street to Al Sahd's Grocery on skid row next to the Lucky Bar and bought a chunk of baloney and a loaf of bread. Then he caught a cab and picked up Anna, whose hair was still in curlers.

"Come on," he said. "I've got to paint you."

"Not like this," she said.

"Like that. Bring the towel to tie around your head." They stopped on skid row again and got two bottles of wine. She posed. He painted. They both drank all night. He painted her with the towel wrapped around her head and with her blouse removed. She had to hold her arms up as if wrapping the towel. Toward morning the cramps came in her shoulders, and every few minutes she'd drop her arms.

"Please forgive me, Saw. I hold as long as I can."

"I know," he said, "just a moment more now. Just a little more, Anna. I don't like to paint by artificial light, but somehow with you I get the colors right anyway."

"When they put your lights back?"

"Last week. It's a good thing I paid. We need them now. Just five minutes more, Anna. That's all, honey."

Anna strained. She knotted her jaws, and her muscles quivered, and millions of needles stuck in her flesh.

"There!"

"You finish?"

"Yes," he said, his own body giving into exhaustion now. He could hardly walk over to the wash basin. "Go home, Anna. I'll see you tomorrow."

"It's already tomorrow."

"Well, later then."

Anna put her blouse on and quietly requisitioned twelve dollars from the pile of money on the bed. She was taking no chances. Shaw might get drunk and spend all the money. She slipped out into the cold darkness.

Shaw fixed coffee and fought himself to stay awake. It was very difficult, especially after the sun came up. But he had to somehow. He walked around the room and stopped and stared at the painting. After eons of time the sun reached ten o'clock. He splashed his face with ice water and dried it briskly. Then he took the wet painting and headed for the Taos Inn.

As he crossed the street he saw a policeman step out of the lobby door. A man in plain clothes was followed by his friend from the day before and another plain-clothes man. His friend was handcuffed between them. They marched briskly to the sidewalk.

A sickness struck at Shaw's whole body.

"Where are you going with him?" he shouted, running in front of them.

"Out of the way," one man said firmly but politely.

"Where are you taking him? He is a nice man. Don't you know that?" He shouted, "He knew I was in need without my telling him! He gave without my asking! Don't you understand what that means?"

"Get out of the way," the state trooper said, "or I'll put you under arrest as well."

"But I did this for him," Shaw said, holding the painting up, trying to get them to look. "I worked all night so he could enjoy it today."

"Move over," they said and walked by. "You can send it to him in care of Huntsville Prison."

Shaw dropped the painting in the gutter without realizing it.

"No," he said softly. "No. No." He walked dazedly through the lobby and up to the bar. The words of Holt reached his ears.

"It's hard to believe. He's an accountant from Houston. He embezzled ten thousand dollars. He knew he was caught, so he brought his wife and kids out here on a last vacation. He sent them home yesterday afternoon."

"Can you beat that?" someone said.

"You never can tell, can you?" someone else said.

"No, sir, you never can."

"He seemed like a nice enough feller," Holt said.

"That's the kind you better watch. After you've been in this business as long as I have, you learn to watch them all. What can I do for you, Shaw?"

"You can't do a thing for me, Holt. Not a thing. You never could."

Shaw turned and walked out into the street, but he couldn't look down it to where they'd taken the man. He saw the painting in the gutter. A car had run it over and broken the stretchers and smeared the oils into an unrecognizable mess. Kay Miller's new husband would probably love it now. He left it there and went home to bed.

26

ZACHARIAS CARRIED THE SACK under his arm with pride. It was seldom that he had the opportunity to buy a drink for his pardner, Shaw. He knocked on the studio door. There was no answer. He knew what that meant for sure. Shaw had worked on the ceiling all night.

Zacharias yelled, "Yaaa! Pardner, let me in. You hear me, pardner?"

He put his ear against the door and heard a stirring. In a moment the door opened a crack. Zacharias pushed his way in, seeing the uncleaned palette and brushes and two empty wine bottles. Shaw stood pushing his hair back and rubbing his swollen eyes.

"Here," Zacharias said, pulling the bottle of wine from the sack.

Shaw took it and made a bitter face. He took a slug of the maroon juice nevertheless, grimacing and slinging his head. He went over and turned up the small butane heater and put some coffee on an electric burner.

Zacharias warmed his behind by the heater and his insides with the wine. He watched Shaw silently as they waited for the coffee to heat.

As soon as Shaw poured them each a cup and had taken a couple of swallows, Zacharias spoke. He had been pondering whether to use his elevated speech or his stupid Mexican act. Both worked on Shaw. But since it was both a high- and low-class subject he was to speak on, he decided to use the combination approach.

"Pardner, you know, of course, of the great healing powers for the flesh and bone of the waters of Ojo Caliente?"

Shaw nodded.

"Well, has it ever occurred to you why the men of Ojo and the neighboring villages of La Madera and Petaca have such health and vitality?"

"The hot springs?"

"No, my pardner. No. No! Before I answer, let me continue the questions and remarks. Now Ojo is the only area in all of America where the men outlive the women by a great number of years. I read this in the *Albuquerque Journal* last year. Everywhere else the women kill the men off early with the geets."

"The geets?"

"Si, amigo, geet me theece and geet me that. Savvy? At Ojo it is different; the men kill off the women with the gives. They drink the water from a certain spring near La Madera."

"Is it a hot spring, too?"

"No, no. It is cool water, but its power is ten times that of the hot. Now, a pint of this water will make a stallion jump a ten-wire fence."

"An aphrodisiac?" Shaw asked, perking up.

"I don't know about that thing you said, pardner, but it gives the mind many thoughts, all about the same thing."

Shaw grinned and reached for the bottle of wine. "Women!"

"Ahhh, now you have your finger on the truth."

"I appreciate your telling me about this, Zacharias, but I just don't need any help at all. Just a little more time is all."

Zacharias did a small jig. "But of course, neither do I. That Mama," he beamed, "she could make a man break out of jail the way she shakes that big behind." Zacharias became very serious now. "But others with a few more years, perhaps, are not so fortunate as you and I."

"Sell it?" Shaw asked.

"The finger is on the right spot again, amigo. We can bottle it and sell it. At the same time we can do great favors for many. You do much good trading in the gringo bars, pardner. What better product to trade than a gift of love?"

The wine bottle was emptied in full agreement. Zacharias said, "Come get your truck; Mama has been out gathering bottles for us all morning."

Shaw said, "You take the truck and get the bottles while I clean these brushes."

Zacharias looked at the unfinished ceiling, shook his head slightly, and left Shaw to clean his palette and brushes, all the while marveling at the inspiration of his friend.

They drove across the desert west from Taos, where the blue-gray sage carpeted the desert three feet deep. Soon they came to the black sides of the Rio Grande Gorge. They wound down the curving road and past the lava bluffs and out through almost seven hundred feet by the emerald river. They crossed the bridge and wound up the other side and back again to desert, broken here and there by weed-covered fields long ago deserted by farmers for a more promising land. Some had tried the land here. All had failed except the lone little cow outpost, which survived by hauling firewood to Taos from the nearby piñon hills.

They drove to the highway and straight to La Madera, missing Ojo by two miles.

"See that old man there?" said Zacharias, pointing to a house by the side of the road where an old, old man sat in the sun watching several children at play. That's old Mascarenas. His wife died when he was seventy. He married an eighteen-year-old girl and now has six more children. Eighty-seven. That's what the hard water will do for you."

"Hard water?"

"Si, the spring is called Hard Water Spring." Zacharias laughed loudly at this, jigging his feet against the floorboard of the pickup and beating Shaw so happily on the back he almost drove into the Brazos River.

"Here, pool over there." Zacharias got out and opened the gate. Shaw drove through, and when Zacharias got back in the truck, Shaw asked, "You sure we're not trespassing?"

"Si, I'm sure."

"How come it's fenced with six-foot-high sheep wire all around then?"

"AAAAYAA, that is to keep the wild animals from the hard water. One swallow of this, amigo, and a jackrabbit would mount a mule. A field mouse would mount a mountain lion." Zacharias was laughing again so hard he could hardly gasp out, "Stop, this is the place."

They filled the thirty-two bottles, which ranged in size from a jam jar to a one-gallon vinegar jar.

Shaw tasted the musky water.

Zacharias yelled, "Pardner, not now. It's too early. Besides, you don't need it, remember?"

Shaw remembered. They drove back down the Brazos. Zacharias said, "You got any money, pardner?"

"Yeah, four dollars."

"The thought of the hard water has made me thirsty. Maybe a little bottle of wine to soften the long trip home, huh?"

Shaw agreed that the thinking was perfect. So they drove into the village of Ojo and stopped at the first bar.

Zacharias knew the bartender well and greeted him with warmth. "Yaahaa, Adolpho, meet my pardner, Mr. Shaw." They shook hands.

Adolpho said, "What you doin' over here, Zacharias, taking the cure at the spring?"

"What is there to cure, amigo? I have no troubles. We have come to gather the hard water."

"What do you mean you have no troubles, hombre? If you need the hard water you got the worst troubles in the whole son of a beetch world."

"No, no, you do not understand, Adolpho. It is not us that has the problems. Why, Mr. Shaw Spencer is worse than a two-year-old ram, and me, well just look at happy Mama and count my children. We get the water to sell for love and profit."

"Nobody believe you. Only local folks know truth about hard water."

"Mr. Spencer can sell anything. He's an artist, and he even sells pictures in the gringo bars."

Adolpho shoved his fat elbows harder into the bar top, lifting his dumpy head higher, and looked at Shaw with a new and much greater respect.

They bought a bottle of wine with Shaw's money and left.

Adolpho came to the door and yelled after Zacharias, "Now don't go drinkin' up the profits, Zaco. You can't afford the kids you got." They both laughed good-bye.

"A fine man, that Adolpho," said Zacharias, and they passed the bottle back and forth all the way to Taos.

They parked at the studio, and Shaw picked up the sack Zacharias had dropped that morning.

"I'm going into action," he said, and he walked out, leaving Zacharias with a third of a bottle and a sleepy feeling. He went to get Anna, and they both entered the Taos Lounge.

Holt eyed the sack suspiciously. He was hoping it was an antique he could barter for, to the point of considering thievery. An hour or so later he was surprised to see the two bottles of murky water sitting on a table as Shaw was telling two fifty-year-old vice presidents from Amarillo, "And this stuff'll make a field mouse mount a mountain lion."

There was much laugher, and one of the vps said, just as Shaw expected, "It isn't a mountain lion I'm after, friend."

"Let's give it a try," they both said at once.

Shaw had long known just the spot to pinch on Anna's thigh to make her crawl all over him. It was like pushing the button on a dynamo. After an hour of observing this action and reaction of Anna to Shaw, the vps were ready to believe the credibility of the hard water's power.

Holt, who had busied himself behind the bar watching the action, almost stabbed himself with a lemon peeler when the vps handed Shaw a twenty-dollar bill for the two pints of dirty water. For a moment, jealousy chilled Holt, but he warmed at the thought that a good portion of the twenty would be spent across his bar. If one looked carefully there was some benefit to be gained from almost everything.

Now Shaw, Zacharias, and Anna stayed well fed, drunk, and happy for several days. It would be the last of plenty for quite a spell. Finally Shaw could hold off no longer, and he drank the last four bottles in an hour, ran Zacharias out of the house, and told the sleepy-eyed Anna to prepare for battle.

The next day, while driving across the desert with Anna and Zacharias after another supply of water, Anna said, with a solemn face, "Sell it, si. Drink it, no." And she shifted her big bottom around on the seat and said, "Wheehooo."

But the word about a good thing had evidently spread. Someone did, after all, own the Springs, and now there was a new sign up that read, "POSTED—NO TRESPASSING." They suffered a small shock that lasted perhaps forty seconds, and then Zacharias said, looking at Anna, "Well, amigos, we don't really need it. Not us."

So disappeared a new industry in the high mountain air of Taos, New Mexico, USA.

26

ZACHARIAS WALKED INTO SHAW'S STUDIO nowadays without knocking. Lately Shaw could be found sitting upright so sound asleep that he couldn't be awakened by pounding on the door. It seemed that he worked mostly on the ceiling now. He was getting thin from a scarcity of food and his immense battle with the mural. Zacharias had half a bottle of wine and some cheese and crackers. He didn't fully understand why he brought them to Shaw—he was just as hungry as the young artist. But then, Shaw was working harder than he was. The last time he'd come here the canvas ceiling was almost covered. Shaw's face was pulled down, and his skin was tight over his facial features. His eyes were trying to hide in his skull so they couldn't see the world on each side, only the one straight up on the ceiling.

"Ah, amigo," he said, shaking Shaw, who slowly opened his tired, sunken eyes.

"Ah, amigo, a feast. Wake up and let us dine."

Shaw smiled weakly, shoved the eternally falling hair out of his eyes, took a drink of wine, and stuck a piece of cheese between two crackers. He ate it slowly, half-starved but still not hungry.

"I have great news for you, pardner," Zacharias said enthusiastically. "Carlotta the witch told us last night that my check would come tomorrow. And spring is the same as here. All is well." He took another pull of wine and handed it to Shaw.

Shaw raised it to his lips, tasted it, and stared up at the ceiling.

"I see that you have finished the ceiling," Zacharias shouted joyfully. "This is the great one, no, amigo?" And he moved about doing an old Spanish dance. "I'll go get my fiddle and play for you. Everyone is broke, but I'll go rob a store or something. We must celebrate!"

Shaw raised a hand. "It isn't finished yet, Zacharias. It needs one more touch. Just the right highlight."

He rose to his feet, stiffly for so young a man, put a smear of light color on his brush, and walked slowly toward the canvas, staring hypnotically.

Zacharias stood in the middle of the room holding the bottle of wine without putting it to his lips. A great rarity this. He knew the contents were small, and they must be reserved for the finality of this one stroke of the magic brush. He wondered and played a guessing game as to the location of the stroke, and then he saw it was on Anna, just off-center of the canvas. She glowed out at them much stronger than real life. Living, vibrating, pulsating, her eyes dancing like her middle body. There was perfume there, and the essence of all evil and good, and man, and woman and child. The world whirled around her, and the lightning crashed into the mountains behind her, and all the other people in the canvas dimmed. All the bitches, all the Holts, and all the world melted into a fine mist of gold perfume surrounding Anna as Shaw made the one stroke on her breast in the shape of the world.

Shaw just stood, stiff and very old looking.

Zacharias leaped into the air, screaming, yelling. "Viva! Viva! Oh, amigo, I must tell Mama and the children, and all our amigos. It is truly great! I see it all perfectly, like the evening star on a clear night. It is all there! All! What are you doing, pardner?"

Shaw whirled suddenly.

Zacharias, being a man sensitive to the moods of friends, stood pale with his nerves jumping out of his body as Shaw said, "I must make a sacrifice to show the Great Mystery in the Sky that I appreciate all of life, not just my art."

Suddenly his body became young before Zacharias's eyes. The hunger was gone. The lights came on in the sockets of his head, and Zacharias laughed again. He laughed and he laughed, feeling something he couldn't define and was too wise to be foolish enough to try. He took his gray hat off and stomped up and down on it.

Then he laughed some more as Shaw folded his great canvas and shoved it into the stove, stuffed paper around it, and lit a fire to it. Anna and all the other images of the great deserts, mountains, and valleys disappeared in a few puffs of smoke.

Zacharias asked no more questions. He could tell that, as crazy as this appeared, Shaw felt it was right. That was all he needed to know. He slapped Shaw on the back and said, simply, emphatically, "You did it, pardner."

"Yes, I did it, Zacharias. It was all that was good in the whole canvas, but Anna was perfect. A flawless painting of her. It was a part of me, that's all." He rolled the words on his tongue like a fine wine turned cheap. "I could never show it to anyone but you and Anna. I just couldn't, that's all. Now that it's gone, I have it forever."

"Si, amigo. Now you know what you are. Come, let us go lie and steal and celebrate all our good fortune."

They walked out of the studio. Shaw was almost as jaunty in his stride as Zacharias Chacon, who to all should be henceforth and forever known as the King of Taos. True royalty.

28

SPRING IS HARD TO BEAT IN TAOS. Partly because the frigid winters last so long. The snow melts in the high mountains and courses down all the creeks in tumbling, muddy movement toward the Rio Grande, but the streams soon settle and turn cool, clear, and pure. The livestock would run themselves poor trying to get a mouthful of the green grass now shooting up between the brown, dead stems of winter. In a month, though, they could fill their bellies in an hour and rest in the sun. The birds sang a little but were still wary of some trick of nature.

All over town a movement was on. People were preparing for summer, repairing shops, moving things about, and wondering what the tourist trade would be this summer season.

The winds milled around the Resting Place, and the winos were trembling from their years of drinking. But even so it was better to tremble from alcohol alone than drink and cold combined.

Zacharias sat on the drinking pole. Romo was still in school. There was no way for him to earn his father a bottle's worth of money. Mama couldn't get paid for her ironing until tomorrow. It seemed that all his friends were broke.

Indian Tony had walked across the street to a stranger and said, "Dear brudder, give me eighteen cents, please. I must catch taxi to pueblo, my seester she sick with shakes."

The stranger handed it over, glancing around to see if anyone was watching.

Indian Tony headed straight to the bar and had a glass of fifteen-cent wine. That left only three cents among them all.

There were two other Indian Tonys in Taos of much distinction.

Tony Reyna was on the Bataan Death March and had survived terrible torture and near starvation for many years in a Japanese prison. He had returned to be elected Taos Pueblo governor and had put a profitable and notable curio shop on the road to the pueblo.

Then there was Tony Lujan of Taos Pueblo, who had married the world-famous doyenne of the arts, Mable Dodge. He was not only a great entertainer for Mable's world-famous friends, but many of the artists did paintings and black-and-white drawings of him. He was thought of as a great model in many ways. Mabel Dodge used him to entice many world-famous people—such as Georgia O'Keeffe and D. H. Lawrence and his wife, Frieda—to add to the legends of this tiny town of Taos, New Mexico.

The Indian Tony of the Taos streets was just as skilled but known by only a few of his grape-loving amigos.

Juandias, the Woodhauler, was thinking too. The selling of firewood was over now for several months, and he would never again be tied to the mountains. He would have to devise other methods of subsistence without Patrociño Barela in search of cedar for his carvings; he would miss that as well.

The Undertaker thought of Matias Chacon. The Iron One's funeral had been a good one, but it had not fulfilled him any more than Patrociño's had. He watched Matias standing facing the sun, his swollen face expressionless. Matias would count now and then, duck, and attempt to raise his hands in combat. Yes, it was up to the Fighter now to satisfy him. He was next in line. No doubt about it, another beating would surely finish him.

And then it happened!

The Lover came running with Rosita right behind, holding her bouncing pregnancy with both hands.

"Papa," she screamed, "Papa, it's here! It came at last, Papa!"

"We're rich," cried the Lover. "Look!" He pulled the long blue check from the envelope and handed it to Zacharias.

All gathered around. Zacharias was not fully aware of what was happening yet. He'd waited so long that it failed to register. He held the check and stared. All waited. Nothing happened. He stared as if in shock, which of course he was. Then the check began to shake violently in his hands, and Zacharias fell off the pole backward in a faint.

"Papa!" Rosita yelled, and she knelt uncomfortably by him, taking his cold face in her hands. "Papa, don't die now. We're rich, dear Papa."

Juandias, the Woodhauler, being no fool, raced into the liquor store, leaped up on the counter, grabbed a bottle from the shelf, and, with the screams of the proprietor pounding his ears, raced back outside. He took the cap from the bottle with his teeth and, crowding his way to Zacharias's side, rammed it into his mouth. It was drink or drown for Zacharias. He drank.

Soon the natural color—a deep rose flush—returned to his face. He choked and swallowed valiantly. He sat up. He looked again at the check. Then he rose up, hurling Rosita and everyone aside, and just flew into the air. He yelled. Each time he came down he yelled. Each time he leaped high he yelled. He ran into the liquor store and shouted, "A hundred pints of Tokay for Juandias, the Woodhauler."

It took some time for the proprietor to examine the check and the enclosed letter and decide it was good. He could only supply thirty bottles of the Tokay that Juandias loved, but that was enough for the present.

"Go get my business pardner," he cried at the Lover. "Bring my business pardner here. He'll know what to do!"

They all gathered around the Resting Place and tried to drink some out of each of the thirty bottles. Never in their lives had they had more than they could possibly drink in two days.

Shortly the Lover returned with Shaw.

"Look!" shouted Zacharias, handing a bottle and the check at the same time into Shaw's hands.

"Thirty-six thousand dollars back compensation," Shaw read. "Come with me, Zacharias. You must get this in the bank before something happens to it."

So the entire entourage moved across the street and around the corner of the plaza into the bank. The invasion, being unheralded and unannounced, created considerable excitement. The clerks raised their heads and started slinging them about, for they knew not what to do.

The customers broke up the lines and turned around to watch the activities.

As Shaw marched forward with the check, one teller yelled, "Hey, you can't drink on these premises. Here now, put all those bottles away. Do you know what you are doing? Will I have to call the law?"

But nothing prevailed. The joy was too great. Shaw took care of the deposit. The teller locked the door until all was done. Then they pridefully strode out, looking at the brand-new checkbook Zacharias held in his hand.

"You mean, Shaw, all I have to do is sign my name here, and I get money?"

"Yes, but remember how I showed you to fill in the amounts with writing and numerals, or someone could take all your money."

"I'll remember," swore Zacharias.

First Zacharias wrote out a check for two hundred dollars, which he dispensed among his friends. He felt that should do them for the day since they had thirty bottles of wine to go on already. Well, twenty and a half now.

"Go get Mama," he cried to Rosita. "Get all the babies. Come to the Yucca Store with me."

In the meantime Shaw and Zacharias went over to the Ford Garage and bought a new pickup from Mr. Harper. Since the only thing he cared about was the color—green—they had not a bit of trouble or wasted time.

"We'll need this to haul all Mama's presents today," said Zacharias, suddenly feeling and acting in a businesslike manner. "Later we can use it in our construction business. Now go call the bulldozer company and buy us a tractor, Shaw."

Shaw did as he was asked. He put in a call to the Lively Equipment Company in Albuquerque. He'd met and had a few drinks with a nice fellow who sold for them. His name was Jim John Beck. Shaw always found him pleasant, intelligent, and full of fun. He insisted on talking to Beck.

"Beck?" Shaw asked. "You may not remember me. This is Shaw Spencer from Taos."

"Yeah, Shaw. We had some good times in the Taos Inn. How are you?"

"Good. Listen, how much for a D6 tractor?"

"New or used?"

"Well . . . used, I guess."

"Yeah, well I have a good used one for seven thousand cash."

"Sounds fine. Bring it up, will you?"

"Are you serious?"

"Of course. I'm buying it for Zacharias Chacon. It's for cash. Have your company call the bank if necessary."

"All right, Shaw. I'll have it serviced, and we'll come up with it sometime tomorrow afternoon."

"That'll be fine, Beck. We'll wait out on the highway at the Sleeping Boy. You know where that is, don't you?"

"You mean Cunico's Curio and Bar on the south side of town?"

"That's it. He's got plenty of parking space in front for everything."

"Okay, we'll meet you there."

Shaw met the Chacon family at the Yucca Builders. Zacharias ordered new beds for Rosita and her babies, an ironing board, and a new refrigerator and matching freezer for Mama. He bought saws, hammers, curtains, a living-room suite, and a new TV set.

"Let's go to the JCPenney store," he shouted, taking a nice, clean swallow of Tokay and passing the bottle.

He bought a whole rack of dresses for Mama, and when she protested that some might not fit, he said, "It doesn't matter. Rosita or the babies can wear them. We don't have time to wait."

Everyone had to have a pair of new shoes, including Shaw. Trying them on took a few minutes, even though Zacharias swore that each pair fit perfectly regardless of size.

The Lover drove the pickup load of dresses, coats, and other assorted items home and returned to the supermarket, where the family had now gathered.

Zacharias insisted that everyone get a push basket. He did the honors.

"Here, Shaw, three hams for you. Ten chickens for you, Mama. Only bacon for you, Rosita." He laughed. "You're too fat now. Here, Mama, do you like pineapple?"

Mama was now in such a condition that she just followed along and nodded her head at every question and statement. She no longer had much of her reasoning left. He took the entire shelf of pineapple cans and called for a delivery boy to help. Soon there were three delivery boys taking load after load to the checkers and from there to the pickup.

"Ahhh," Zacharias cried, "oranges! I have never had enough oranges." So he bought all three bushels.

"Papa," Mama said. "I like these pretty flowers."

"Those? But they have no smell. Mama, they are silk."

"Yes, I know, Papa. But I like them. They are pretty forever."

"Well, then, let's take them all!" he said, and he started gathering them up by the armful. "You and Rosita take the groceries home. Be sure and stop by Shaw's and leave his hams and stuff. We're going now to the Cantina. Come," he said grandly, and he grabbed Mama around the waist.

The manager of the store was wringing his hands, half in delight and half in fear. "Mr. Chacon, Mr. Chacon, the check please." All business had stopped. It had taken all three cash registers going full blast to check everything.

"Oh yes, the check." In truth Zacharias hadn't known who the manager was talking to. This was the first time in his life he could remember being called mister.

He wrote out the check and handed it to the manager.

"Thank you, Mr. Chacon. Come again, sir."

They marched to the Cantina in full force, and such a party hadn't been seen in Taos since the days of the fur trappers and the mountain and mining men. The message had spread in the manner no one understands, and by dark the place was so full that there was hardly room to pass out. Mama didn't let this faze her. She went to sleep in the booth next to Zacharias with a stunned smile engraved on her face. She dreamed of the new refrigerator. It was full of all sorts of delicious food for her beloved family. All Mama's conscious thoughts were always on what was best for her loved ones, and so were her sleeping dreams.

Zacharias sent someone to Canon to get two old musicians. He decided it was his time to sit and listen. The old men came and played. When they were handed twenty dollars apiece after the first song, they almost burned the guitar and violin strings.

Later in the night, when the unconscious could be stacked and sorted against the wall, room was made for dancing. Anna spun and wheeled, shook and shimmied, doing the Tahitian amid great and happy throated yells. Shaw joined her, and the two of them whirled and jumped until both fell sprawled on the floor, laughing until they felt tears roll across their faces.

The revelry continued until the closing hour, and afterward it continued down the streets. The jails were full of merrymakers, the alleys were full of merrymakers, and all were full of merrymaking wine. The day of the check had been a dinger.

29

THE AMIGOS HAD NO CHANCE for a hangover the next day. Zacharias, Shaw, Indian Tony, the Undertaker, the Lover, Anna, and Juandias, the Woodhauler, sat in Johnny Cunico's Sleeping Boy and waited for the delivery of the bulldozer. They waited in comfort and with sufficient libations to calm their nerves.

About two in the afternoon the truck pulled up in front, parallel to the highway.

"There it is, Shaw. Our tractor," exclaimed Zacharias, lunging for the door.

John Beck was introduced to Zacharias, and in a moment the decision had been made about where to unload it. "I can wait no longer," Zacharias said. "I must drive it. I must test it."

"The check," Shaw said, and Zacharias wrote out the check for the amount on the bill.

The truck followed them slowly and turned off to the vacant lot around the old cottonwood tree. It took a while to unload it. Zacharias touched it all over, gently, lovingly, and then he bent and smelled it. The new grease and paint was like Egyptian perfume to him.

He climbed aboard and sat looking at the controls and feeling majestic, like the commander of a battleship.

"Go," he said. "All of you go up the street, and I will drive by you."

Beck said to Shaw, "He's not going to drive this down the highway is he?"

"Oh, I don't think so," said Shaw, so full of wine and wonderment that he really didn't hear what Beck said.

So everyone crowded either in the front or the back of the new green pickup, and Shaw drove the short distance to the Lucky Bar.

Shaw explained, "He just doesn't want anyone around while he tries it out. It's been a long time since he's driven one, and he would be embarrassed if he made a blunder in front of his friends."

Zacharias fired it up, listened to the hum of the mighty motor, and felt the slight quivering of anxious power in its frame. Then he moved it into gear. The blade was lifted. He circled the tree a couple of times.

"Let's get the hell out of here," the truck driver said to Beck. They left, glad they had the check.

Zacharias wheeled the tractor about like a lion fighting a pack of dogs. He dropped the blade, and the rippers on each end bit into the dirt. He plowed a wide furrow through the broken glass. He took a long pull at the bottle and suddenly headed for the highway. This was his machine, this was his dream he held in his fists. This was his moment in all eternity. He raised the blade again as he struck the highway.

Up the street at the Lucky Bar Zacharias's amigos had just put the first glass of wine to their lips when they heard the noise. It was coming closer. All stopped their movements and listened a moment.

"Oh, no!" Shaw said.

They crowded the door. Up the hill toward the crossroads of the plaza it came. It loomed larger with each clang of the treads. It seemed bigger than a five-story building. It was a monster that lived by tearing and mashing. Cars pulled over, dodging the tractor as it moved from side to side like a drunk man. So far Zacharias had struck nothing.

It was near now, almost in front of the Cantina. They could see Zacharias's wide smile as he raised the bottle and emptied it and, as usual, tossed it over his head where it crashed against the street. The tractor treads were doing considerable damage where they dug into the pavement. He was right in front of them now, and that's the first anyone noticed the Fighter.

Matias stepped out in front of the tractor with his hands up and his head against his left shoulder. He was bobbing and weaving. He threw a feint forward with a left hand, and then he tossed a feeble little right across, against the blade of the tractor. His momentum, as weak as it was, carried him forward. His head struck the blade of the tractor. He went down and under the treads. The tractor moved on over him, unfeeling, up the street.

All were paralyzed for a moment.

The Undertaker ran and knelt by the flattened figure where he was ground into the pavement. Only the arms remained whole. He was spread like a Catholic cross.

The Undertaker was crying now. "Matias, you did it for me. Just for me." Tears came out of his eyes as if out of the holes of a rusty bucket. "Ah, at last. Now I can have the funeral Zacharias promised. It will be mine. Totally mine." He picked up Matias's hand, and the arm came off at the elbow. He held it up to his cheek. "Bless you, Matias. It will be a beautiful funeral. I promise. You can depend on me, Matias."

Zacharias turned onto the plaza. He was having difficulty trying to keep the mighty machine off the street.

Zacharias sat enraptured, trying to figure out the reverse gears now. But the police pulled him from the tractor and took him to jail, where he fell fast asleep the instant he hit the floor. The occupants paid him no mind. They had seen it all many times.

A crowd gathered around the remains of Matias. When the ambulance arrived, the drivers had to go across the street to Cantu's Hardware and get a shovel to get all of Matias from the road.

The Undertaker fought with them for the privilege, screaming, "Zacharias promised me! He said I could do it all!"

The ambulance loaded the Undertaker and the canvas-sacked body of Matias at the same time. With the siren screaming they took the Undertaker to the Holy Cross Hospital. He was unconscious on arrival. Then they took the remains of the Fighter to the mortuary.

The Undertaker died that night without awakening. His liver had turned to quartz, and a poison had set in. The winos gave them a double funeral and buried them side by side, friends and companions forever.

Zacharias was sentenced to five weeks in jail. He was out in three weeks for good behavior and told Mama, "It was not all bad except for missing the wine, and soon that didn't matter. Then I missed you most of all, Mama."

Mama held him tight and showed him a big surprise. It was a new steam iron she'd been trying to save for six months to get. Being free for once of the price of Zacharias's wine, it was easy to earn the purchase price.

During the time Zacharias was in jail, the Lover made love to everything he could find. He told himself it was good to be free of Zacharias's observation. He might as well take advantage of the situation so that someone would derive some benefit from it.

He was bothered some by impotency, especially when he was drinking, which was most of the time. This only spurred him on to greater efforts. During the wide dispersal of his charms, he caught a venereal disease. It so weakened him before he knew what was wrong that he tried to kill himself with a dull knife. The blade only penetrated about half an inch through the skin of his chest, causing a painful but not mortal injury.

A short while before Zacharias was freed, Shaw sat in the Cantina, happy at the news his friend would be out of jail in two more days, and watched with loving interest as Anna worked.

She was with an old merchant from an outlying village. He sat in the booth nodding his head as she danced in front of him. He tried to clap and yell now and then, but he couldn't get one hand to hit the palm of the other, and when he opened his mouth to give a happy yell, his teeth dropped and there exuded only a click, a sort of grunt.

Sensing his condition, Anna pushed him over and sat next to him. He felt the inside of her thigh and tried to get his hand further up her dress. She leaned to him and put her cheek against his face so he couldn't see her other hand. There were some bills scattered on top of the table. She quickly gathered them up in a wad while his head was averted. Soon his hand stilled and slipped from her lap as his head dropped over on his chest.

Shaw let out his breath and smiled to himself, pleased. Anna had scored without having to turn a trick.

As soon as she was sure the old one was sound asleep she came and sat by Shaw. She ordered two glasses of wine.

Indian Tony came in and stopped in front of them. "Dear sister," he said, "dear brudder. It is sad to think of our friend Zacharias's troubles. Dear sister, I thirst with a cold. Could you buy me a little drink to make it better? Also, my eye hurt for cold." He rubbed his eye and sniffled the best he could.

Anna nodded to the bartender. He poured a glass for Tony. The Native American took the entire contents of the glass in one swallow.

"I sorrow about our friends, dear sister and brudder," he said.

"There is no need for that, Tony," Shaw said, and he took the rest of the money out of Anna's hand and bought a fifth of Tokay wine. "Come," he said. "I'll paint you both today."

They walked down the street, the three of them. The Mexican whore, the blanket Indian, and the gringo artist.

Yes, that's what he wanted to be—an artist. What could he complain about? He had his two favorite models and a full bottle of wine.

They staggered up the crooked streets of Taos to Shaw Spencer's studio, and they made a toast to Zacharias Chacon, the king with no need for a crown, who would join them very soon. This thought made them all feel much better instantly.